MR. FIXIT

A SEXY ROMANTIC COMEDY

LAUREN LANDISH

Edited by

VALORIE CLIFTON

MR. FIXIT

BY LAUREN LANDISH

He's good with more than just his hands.

I've known Caleb Strong for over a year. We have a special kind of friendship—we make crude comments, double entendres, and tease each other mercilessly.

But we've never crossed that line. We're just friends.

Until we start working together to renovate my childhood home.

Seeing him shirtless working out in the sun is making me want something more. The way his corded forearms twist every screw, the way his biceps flex as he swings his hammer... I want to feel what that brute strength can do to me.

I know once we cross that line, there's no turning back.

But I won't deny it anymore, I want him to make a move.

I have needs, and he's got the tool for the job.

We can still be friends after, right? It'll just be casual.

Until it isn't…

Join my mailing list and receive 2 FREE ebooks! You'll also be the first to know of new releases, sales, and giveaways.

Irresistible Bachelor Series (Interconnecting standalones):
Anaconda || Mr. Fiance || Heartstopper
Stud Muffin || Mr. Fixit || Matchmaker
Motorhead || Baby Daddy

PROLOGUE

CASSIE

"*Y*ou sure about this?" Nathan asks me in his distinct Bronx accent as the muted sounds of the club preparing to open surround us. In the six months I've worked here at Club Jasmine, he's been my boss, a mentor of sorts, and an ear to bend when I need it. He's crude and he's foul-mouthed, but he's honest.

"I'm sure," I reply, tugging at the collar on my work outfit. Tonight is supposed to be 'upscale night', which for the patrons means suits and dresses that hit at least the mid-thigh, and if you have a collar, you'd better be rocking a tie. For me and the rest of the staff, it means a tailored blouse that highlights what boobs I do have, although since it buttons up most of the way to my neck, I can get a little bit extra out of my Wonderbra. "It's time for me to move on."

Nathan sips his drink, a horrible neon blue concoction called a *Little Mermaid* that he can't get enough of. To me, it smells too much like fake fruity wannabe tropical stuff, and I've had the real thing. There's no substitution. "I can respect that," he says after a moment. "We all knew this was just a temporary gig until you figured out what you wanted to do. I didn't expect you to change your mind and make a career here."

I laugh, nodding. "You're right, but it was fun while it lasted."

"We're going to miss you around here. You're popular with the customers. You've got a natural charm about you," Nathan admits. He once asked me out for a drink after work, and while he's an interesting fella, I don't date my boss. I'm not going to hate on anyone who does, but it's not how I want to make my way. Luckily, he took it well and it's never been awkward, just totally cool since then. "So, what are you looking at doing?"

"Similar to what I was doing before, in real estate, but not some corporate setting. A more close-knit group that my friend, Hannah's, husband set up. It's his brother's business."

"Oliver? We've met. He's a good man. I can respect that," Nathan says. He stands up, offering me his hand. "Tell you what—you do me a favor tonight, and I'll even give you a goodbye present, an extra week's pay to get you moved and started."

I raise an eyebrow. Nathan's nice, but he's about as tight-fisted as Ebenezer Scrooge. "What's that?"

"Roxy's grandmother is coming in tonight," Nathan says, and I have to both laugh and wince at the same time. Ivy Jo is . . . unique. "Yeah, well, she insists that she can see her great grandbabies and enjoy a night on the town too, and Jake don't wanna listen to it no more. I can dig it. So, she's coming in early bird."

"How long, and what time?" I ask Nathan, who shrugs.

"Jake told me he'd try to get her out of here by nine, but last time she came in, she threatened to take her cane to my head if I pressured her toward the door one more time," Nathan says defensively. "But Jake and Roxy both say she liked you. As Roxy's getting ready for her set, and Jake's at home playing proud papa, I figure you can make sure she doesn't get into too much trouble tonight?"

I laugh again, nodding. "I'll make sure she doesn't get too out of control."

Two hours later, Ivy Jo comes in, escorted by one of the security guys. "Miss White, Ivy Jo—"

"Oh hell no, that Nathan didn't give me no chaperone, did he?" Ivy Jo protests, decked out in an outfit that . . . well, I think it was popular during the disco era. "I said I wanted a night out, not a night being handheld!"

"Ivy Jo, I'm not your chaperone," I protest, giving her just a little bit of sass. It keeps her on her toes. "I'm here to protect all the men from you. I know how you are, remember?"

"I remember. I remember your being almost as much fun as I was at your age," she says. "Okay, I guess."

I get her a drink, a watered down Rob Roy that she sips at, sighing happily. "Get yourself a drink, girl!"

"Sorry, can't while on the clock," I tell her, "but if you don't mind, I'll go for something virgin."

"I'd like a virgin too, but at my age, I'll take any damn thing I can get," Ivy Jo cackles, and I have to snicker. I get myself a Moscow Mule mocktail and sit down next to her as the early clubgoers start to come in and the DJ starts spinning tunes. "So, talked with Mindy the other day. She said you're going to work for Oliver?"

"Yep," I agree, sipping my mule and wishing it had just a bit more ginger flavor. "Oli's got a place for me. And I'm gonna earn it too. I plan on working my ass off."

"No doubt," Ivy Jo says. "Hey, what about that tall drink of sexy you were teasing all over the damn place when we all went out to Hawaii? What's his name—Calvin?"

"Caleb!" I say with a laugh. Caleb Strong is many things, but I could never, ever imagine him being named Calvin. "What about him?"

"Doesn't he work for Oliver too?" Ivy Jo says with a twinkle in her eye. "You two looked like you got along well."

"We got along like cats and dogs, but we had fun. That's about it though," I reply, not admitting to her that yeah, I've sometimes thought about having a different kind of fun with Caleb. "He still kind of works for Oliver, but he started his own thing, Strong Services, although he's mostly known as 'Mr. Fix-It' to his customers."

"Handy, huh? I used to be a girl who was very much into

handys," Ivy Jo says, making me half choke on my drink. "You sure that drink is virgin?"

"I'm sure," I say with a laugh. "But no, there's nothing there. I haven't seen him since the wedding, and we mostly just send each other inappropriate jokes and memes these days. We're just friends."

"Uh-huh," Ivy Jo says, unconvinced. "Honey, in all my years, I ain't saying that men and women can't be *just friends*. But I saw the sparks between you two, and two people who start off in the friend zone with those sparks either hate each other eventually or . . ."

"Or what?"

Ivy Jo finishes off her Rob Roy, grinning. "I won't ruin it for you. Hell, maybe I'm wrong. Let's go find me a man a third my age to shake my hips with. Left one's brand new. Gotta get some use outta it before the rest of me breaks down!"

CHAPTER 1

CALEB

*S*weat stings my eyes as I reach down into the hole, working by feel. I could have dug something wider. I know quite a few of the contractors around town who damn near rip up an entire back yard for a job like this, but that's not me. I take a lot of pride in my work, and that includes creating as little collateral damage as I can.

"Come on, you stupid son of a—" I grunt, twisting the connector to the right. I've only got a tiny window, and I have to reset after just a moment, evaluating my progress as I do. Not bad. A few more and I'll have it done.

I reach down again, but just as I do, my earbud works itself loose and I curse under my breath. Sitting up, I use the opportunity to wipe my forehead, but it's just too hot. To hell with it. I take my other earbud out and pull my t-shirt off, whipping it around my head in a quick do-rag-like getup that looks stupid as hell, but at least it keeps my eyes clear. I readjust my earbuds and the thrilling, driving voice of Roxy Stone fills my ears. It's not a CD yet—she's still working on the final arrangements—but I've been able to listen to all of her covers as she works on them. Advantages of being a friend of the family, and her version of *Hallelujah* fucking rocks.

My adjustments complete, I reach down and twist the wrench again, then again. Grabbing my flashlight, I look the whole thing over, from the pipe tape I used on the threads right down the pipe itself. "That oughta hold you," I mutter, getting to my knees. I go over to the side of the house, turning the water back on, and head back to the ditch, squatting down and staring intently at my repair. The pipe's good, no leaks at all, and I quickly finish up, filling in the dirt and tamping it down before putting the turf back on top as best I can. Packing my bag, I look over the whole job, nodding in approval. "Nice," I tell the afternoon cicadas as I take off my earbuds and put them in the pocket of my work jeans. "Mrs. Barnes is going to have no problems with water leaks or her petunias for the rest of the summer at least."

I dust off my hands and pick up my tool bag before heading to the back door of the small but trim cottage house that I've been working outside of for the past four hours. Knocking on the frame next to the screen, I take a moment to admire the blue house with white trim, while at the same time noting that a lot of the trim on the north side of the house is looking sun-faded. It might need to be redone soon. "Mrs. Barnes? I just finished up!"

There's the sound of sandals flapping, and a soft voice calls from inside. "Come on in, Caleb!"

"I dunno, Mrs.—"

"Don't worry about the dirt. I insist!" Mrs. Barnes says. She's a widow. Her husband died two years ago, and this is the third job I've done around her place. She just never picked up any do-it-yourself skills beyond the basics. "My husband never worried about it, and I'm mopping the kitchen this evening after dinner anyway!"

Shrugging, I put my bag down just outside the door and step inside. I find Mrs. Barnes on the other side of the kitchen, wearing a tennis skirt outfit. For a woman who's probably in her sixties, she definitely stays active. Maybe she's on her way out to play. "Looks like your petunias are safe for the rest of the summer, Mrs. Barnes," I say after carefully wiping my feet. "That new PVC pipe is going to last you for years."

"Thank you, Caleb," she says. I notice that she's touched up her blonde hair and makeup too as she turns, holding out a big glass of lemonade and a plate of cookies for me. "You looked like you were working like a total draft horse out there. How about a few cookies?"

I smile shyly. I can't help it. I know what she's doing, and it's really beginning to embarrass me. I take the glass and drink. The woman does make a pretty kick-ass glass of lemonade, with real lemon juice that she squeezes by hand and a few other secret tricks that she says she won't tell me, just that it's 'something men wouldn't understand'. It's nearly ice cold too, tart and sweet and singing as it rolls down my throat. I have to be careful. It's so cold that I know if I chug like I want, I'm going to end up with a splitting headache, and I don't want that. Setting the glass down, I take one of her homemade peanut butter cookies and take a bite. "Thank you, Mrs. Barnes."

"You're so very welcome, Caleb," she says, setting the plate down. "Oh dear, I do hope this wasn't a good shirt?"

She reaches out, putting a well-manicured hand on my arm, and I see the small tear in my t-shirt. It's new, probably from when I tied the thing around my head, but I shrug, feeling weird. I don't want to be rude, and I don't want to upset a nice lady who's a good customer, but I'm not interested in her 'features'. Also, not to put too strange a point on it, you just don't seduce a man like me with lemonade and peanut butter cookies. It's the sort of thing she'd give her son if the son of a bitch didn't live in Bend, Oregon, and work as a regional coordinator for FedEx. He didn't even come home for his father's funeral.

Doesn't make it any less weird, and I chew my cookie quickly, trying to keep things professional. "Mrs. Barnes, if you'd like, I'll mail you the invoice for the work today—"

"Nonsense, Caleb, you just rest yourself right there and I'll go get my checkbook. You do take checks, right?" she asks, even though she already knows the answer, but I nod anyway. With most of my customers being from an earlier generation, I've gotten used to taking checks more than cash or credit cards. "I really do have to thank Janice for recommending your services. You are quite the Mr. Fix-It." She emphasizes each word like she has something besides irrigation pipes for me to fix . . .

I chuckle. I don't mind my nickname. "Thanks."

While she fills out the check, I eat another cookie, getting the balance just right. Eat too many, and she's going to insist that I stay longer and have some more because apparently, I need the calories. Eat too few, and I offend her. I swear, I learned more about how to do customer relations in the social hour after church than I ever did in college. When Mrs. Barnes comes back, she glances at the plate of cookies and mostly empty glass of lemonade, giving me another smile and a pat on the chest. "Really, Caleb, you are a godsend. I didn't know what to do when I suddenly started gaining a new swamp out in the back yard. And coming over on your Saturday? I appreciate it. You must have some young lady that you're standing up to take care of me."

I shake my head, smirking. "No, Mrs. Barnes. I was only planning on catching Mindy's new frappe and listening to some new music. I was able to do the music, and I'll grab the frappe later."

"Well, I'll certainly tell all of my friends about you," she says. "Mr. Fix-It is going to be in high demand around here."

I smile, backing away and heading out the door. I don't want to run, even though the hungry look in her eye tells me I probably should. Giving her a little wave, I grab my tool bag and walk around the side of her house to my work truck, a ten-year-old Silverado that I just got a new paint job for. I hate looking like a 'handyman', even if it is my job, and I make sure my truck looks good. When Mrs. Barnes taps on the front window and gives me another wave, I break into what I can only call a power walk, half throwing my tool bag into my cargo box before jumping behind the wheel and backing out as fast as I safely can. "That's it," I mutter to myself as I narrowly avoid her mailbox. "I'm backing into everyone's driveway from here on out."

I drive away, chuckling to myself as I reach the stop sign and turn right, heading for the gas station. Really, scared of an old lady who was just feeling a little 'autumn heat'? Getting out, I top off the tank—I never let my truck get below a half tank after running out of gas in high school— and lean back, laughing to myself. I guess I'm more tired than I thought. Or maybe the lemonade was a little harder than normal?

Nah, that's not Mrs. Barnes's style. Like a lot of my clients, she's pretty sweet. I didn't think she'd be one of the flirty ones at first, but I've gotten my fair share of customers who want to put a little spice in their lives by calling me over to do work around their houses. I didn't expect that, but it's okay.

It still sometimes feel like I stumbled into this line of work by lucky accident. When my best friend, Tony Steele's, mother had us do some work for her, I was glad to help Tony out. After he left town to take over a new family venture in Hawaii, I was asked by his big brother, Oliver, to join him at Steele Solutions. While I'm more than happy to help Oliver out in town and around the area, I'm no real estate tycoon type. I like working with my hands and my brain at the same time. Rewiring a house, repairing plumbing, all sorts of things like that are more interesting to me than just running numbers on a computer screen.

Not that I don't give Oliver his respect. The man works hard, and he's hardly the kind to sit on his ass. His business, his family, his wife's cafe . . . the man works hard, and he can use his hands as much as his brain when he wants. But for me, I get as much satisfaction out of fixing a roof as I do cashing the check I get for the job. Oliver just likes to separate the two is all.

"That way, he doesn't get hit on by his customers," I chuckle as I put the nozzle away. "But I gotta remember to thank him and his mom."

It's true. Janice Steele's word, and her circle of friends, have made it possible for me to be an independent handyman. Starting with working around her place, then Oliver's properties in town, I've grown to the point that I'm booked out sometimes two weeks in advance, unless it's an emergency job like Mrs. Barnes's garden. Most of my customers, other than Oli, who's more than willing to jump in and swing a hammer with me if he can, are either widowed or have husbands who are getting up there in age, and they aren't quite up to some of the challenges of keeping up a house. That's where I come in.

I climb back into my truck, heading for home. It's not a big place, a fixer-upper that I bought with the 'finder's fee' check that Oli cut me for the Hawaii property he's made huge bank on, but I've got it in good shape after a year. Either way, I've got the rest of the weekend to chill out, then Monday, it'll be back to work. "Ah, it's not all bad," I tell myself as I head out, plugging my music player into the dash of my truck and letting Roxy's voice accompany me home. "Eight hours a day, five days a week, and I'm my own boss. TLC for Oli's properties, repair jobs, and cashing checks. Can't really beat that."

"Well, there's one way I could beat it," I think as Roxy switches to one of her love ballads. "But that's not for me."

CHAPTER 2

CASSIE

"*A*nd boom!" I cheer myself as, with a bump of my hip, I close the filing cabinet drawer, signaling another project complete. "Headshot!" I hit the button on my computer's media player, and a karaoke version of the old DMX song *X Gon' Give It To Ya* starts playing, with me singing my own version instead. "Cass gon' give it to ya, fuck doin' deals on your own, Cass gon' deliver to ya . . ."

I know my little celebration is trite, and I really shouldn't be yelling out *Headshot* complete with my own choreo-graphed song and dance every time I complete a deal, but I've busted my butt on this. Besides, I'm alone on the second floor of the Flaming Dragon building, and nobody's around to see my silly moves or hear my stupid lyrics. And if Tom Cruise can dance to Ludacris in *Tropic Thunder*, then by God, I'll do what I want when no one can see me.

I'm just hitting the final lines when I turn around and find my boss, Martha, standing inside the door, laughing silently at my antics. I freeze, both hands thrown up in finger pistols, and she laughs harder as the music stops. "Don't worry about me. I'm just investigating the sound of howling strangled cats they were talking about down in the coffee shop."

"You scared the shit out of me!" I hurriedly protest, wiggling and patting my ass. "I might need to do an undie check! You know how dangerous that was?"

"Oh, yeah, you're the most gangster hundred-and-ten-pound girl in the entire state," Martha says with a chuckle. She's dressed as she always is, in a fashionable blouse and slacks combo that, while nowhere near as formal as the clothing I wore when I worked at Aurora, still broadcasts a sense of professional competence that's more than backed up by what she does. The company might be called Steele Solutions, but Martha's as vital to Oliver's success as his own smarts. "What in the world are you doing?"

"Cel-a-brate-ing! The McCormick deal is officially in the books as a win!" I reply, twirling and blowing off my 'guns' before holstering them in their invisible holsters next to my skirt. I still like to wear my sexy office clothes when I can, and Oliver doesn't mind as long as I'm willing to get dirty and throw on a pair of jeans when I need to. And he knows from his own brother's word that I can get my hands as dirty as anyone. "I got the last of the paperwork from the county clerk today, and it's all ours! Well, Oliver's, or, well . . ."

Martha laughs again. "I know what you mean. Great job, Cassie. That was a complex project. I'm proud of you for getting it done on time and on budget. Listen, Oliver's at home for the day. I heard one of the kids is sick. So how about you take off early, relax, and maybe go out to celebrate tonight?"

She finishes her comment with a raised eyebrow and a smirk. I'm happy to get the praise. And the fact is, I've been busting my butt for a long time, trying to make an impact with the company. Really, it's been hard to maintain my reputation as a ditzy party girl when I haven't been out shaking my ass on the dance floor in ages. But since I started working for Oliver six months ago, I feel like I've grown a lot. Best of all, Oliver's noticed it too. The last two projects, he let me, more or less, run completely solo after he signed off on my plans. Sure, Martha was there as a safety net, but I managed all the contractors, sales listing, and price negotiations, and now it was sold, baby, sold!

And Martha's right. The McCormick deal was a complex project. Originally bought by Tony during Tony's 'funk phase', as he calls it, the original plans had Steele Solutions sitting with that turkey of a property around our necks for the next decade. Instead, by finding the right investors —namely, a Chinese company that wanted to gain an American headquarters and needed a big enough property to get the tax breaks—I was able to take advantage of an opening. By setting up the right contractors for them, I was able to flip the property for not just a profit, but a good profit at that.

"Well, I suppose I could use a little bit of relaxation and reward," I reply, leaning against my desk. "Hmmm . . .

what should I get with my sales bonus? Shoes. Definitely those new peep-toe wedges with the ankle-strap ties. Completely impractical, especially in blush pink, but completely gorgeous and well worth the treat as a reward."

"Shoes?" Martha asks, smirking and shaking her head. "I swear, all the smarts you have in that head of yours, and you blow your bonus on shoes?"

"Not just shoes," I reply, biting my lip. "Maybe I'll stop by Victoria's Secret too. The wrapping is sometimes just as important as the present in the box."

"Yes, well, I don't need to know anything about your box," Martha says mock-primly. While she's no prude, she had to deal with both Oliver's and Tony's overactive single libidos for so long, she's had enough. I don't mind. I've been running a pretty epic dry spell anyway. I like to think I can keep things professional. I can still be a ditz—in fact, a lot of people assume I am just from my personality—and I've even used that to my benefit occasionally. But Martha sees through it so she keeps things at a relaxed professional level in the office. Not that I don't miss joking around with Hannah sometimes. "Go on, get out of here before I find some files to shred or something."

"This is Steele Solutions, not the White House," I tease, grabbing my purse. "Thanks, Martha. See you tomorrow."

I head downstairs, grabbing a frappe and a to-go salad from Mindy's Place before heading back to my apartment. It's not much, a one-bedroom half of a duplex, but compared to what I was living in before, it's a damn mansion. I've actually got my own bedroom and living room that are separated by a real wall and not just a folding divider cutting the space in half. Oh, and a bathtub. Oh my God, the luxury of being able to stretch out in my own bathtub whenever I want . . . it's heaven on earth sometimes.

I pop my salad in the fridge and decide that a bath is just what I need. I can do shoe shopping online anyway. None of the shops in town carry the really good brands. Manolos? Try Mano-nolos around this town. Still, I don't mind. It's a small and safe little town. Besides, Amazon is my buddy. So I pour in some bath oil, a gift from Hannah who sent it from Hawaii, the smell instantly relaxing me as I'm reminded of the forest we had to walk through on a constant basis.

In the year since coming back from Hannah and Tony's wedding, I've missed her, even as we've grown closer as friends. Still, she's nearly five thousand miles and six time zones away, which sort of sucks. But the bath oil is nice, and I'm just about to close my eyes when my phone rings. "Well, speak of the devil and she shall appear," I answer, seeing that it's Hannah. "How's life in paradise?"

"Good," Hannah replies, giggling. "But am I really the devil?"

"Only as much as I'm an angel," I tease in reply. "What's going on?"

"Not much," Hannah says before filling me in on the goings on in Hawaii. In addition to her pregnancy, she and Tony are working at adding some rental cottages to the massive property. While the project's still in the initial stages, it's exciting to think about. "Studmuffin told me you closed the McCormick deal. He wanted to say thanks for pulling that albatross off his neck."

"He can reward me with a first-class plane ticket and two weeks in one of those bungalows, and can you please stop calling your husband Studmuffin all the time?" I joke. "Oh, I love the bath oil. Hawaii smells different from any other place in the world. I guess that's why it's a vacation paradise."

Hannah makes a surprised sound. "You're calling me when you're naked in the bathtub?"

"Nope. I'm answering *your* call while I'm naked in the bathtub," I retort. "A small but important difference. Oh, and tell Tony that when I get there, I expect to have two attendants to see to my every need."

"Tell you what, you get out here, and I'll make sure to find some guy you can order around and tease constantly. Speaking of which, how is Caleb?"

"He's been doing okay. Tony's mom has gotten her friends to give him quite a few jobs over the past few months," I tell her, shaking my head. "We go on our weekend runs usually, but he's been so busy with his handyman work that he has to skip it sometimes. Not to mention, it seems like I'm always out doing something for Oliver anyway. You know, real estate investment is more than sitting on your ass behind a computer."

"Says the woman whom I taught everything she knows,"

Hannah laughs. "If it weren't for me, you'd still be running around Aurora and taking weekend trips to the sex toy shop to replace your most recently worn out toy, Elmer."

"Shh," I reply, putting on a dopey accent. "Be vewwy vewwy qwiet. I'm hunting wabbits."

"Yeah, well, I hope you're not needing one anymore," Hannah says, but when I don't answer, she hums. "How long has it been?"

"A bit," I admit. "But come on, Han, it's not *that* bad. I've just not had the time. I'm enjoying working for Oliver, and I want to learn everything I can from him. You know, opportunities like that don't just fall from the sky."

"Yeah, well, you just remember that good men don't fall from the sky either. You gotta go out there and find them," Hannah says.

We finish up the call and I lean back in the water, letting the scent and the warmth wash away days of tension. The fact is, despite coming across as flirty with the opposite sex sometimes, I've been trying to be more low-key since moving to work with Oliver. I want more out of life than a latex toy, that's for damn sure, and while I'm not a saint, I'm not the girl who was using yoni eggs and packing a silver vibrator in her bag anymore either. Even Hannah senses it, I think, and our comments are more for fun than anything else.

Getting out of the bath, I evaluate myself in the mirror. I've let my hair grow longer. It's almost halfway down my back now, and I think it looks good on me, even if it does make me look a little shorter somehow. I change into some lounge around the house-worthy short shorts and a tank top, letting the boobies dangle free. I'm not built like a pinup model, but I make up for it in other ways.

I get my salad and plop down to my one not-so-secret guilty pleasure, reality shows. Whether it's *Real Housewives*, bachelors and bachelorettes looking for love in all the wrong places, or even people wanting to get totally ridiculous motorcycles built, I love them. Tonight, it's *Wedding Dress Hunters*, and while I eat my salad, I smile as the girl on-screen says yes to a poufy princess monstrosity that looks like it came out of a cheap sci-fi movie or something. Whatever floats her boat, I guess.

Finishing my dinner, I pull my laptop into my lap and start searching for potential properties. It was one of the first things that helped Oliver start to place trust in me. I'm always looking for the next deal, and I routinely find potential properties for him. But my next goal is to do a flip from start to finish . . . find the property, research it, renovate it, and sell it on my own. It'll be my little jump forward on Oliver's trusting me to be independent.

I get lost in the listings, and before I know it, it's almost midnight. I click *Save* on a few of the listings that I want to drive by this weekend and crash into bed, happily exhausted. Maybe it's not a night on the town, but I feel like I've accomplished something.

CHAPTER 3

CALEB

"Ugh," I mutter involuntarily with a wince, holding my hand over my mouth. It doesn't help much. I still feel like the stench is a physical blanket that's assaulting my mouth, nose, and eyes to the point I've got tears running down my cheeks. I've got a pretty strong stomach. I've choked down plenty of disgusting stuff in my time, and I have no problem going elbows deep in a clogged toilet if I have to . . . but this is pushing the limits.

The house is a mess—trash in the corners, holes in the walls, a decided slope to the floor from the front of the house to the back, and a wretched putrid smell that seems to be soaked into every square inch of the walls. When the listing said the house was a 'fixer-upper', I think they were being generous. No wonder Oliver got it so cheap.

I pull out my phone, dialing Oliver. He wanted me to give him a call as soon as I could give him a work estimate. While I wait for him to pick up, I try the window next to me, but it's jammed. Gagging, I head to the back door, but the metal screen door is stuck until I put my boot on the lock and break it off. Fuck it, that's the least of the concerns for this place.

"Hey, Caleb, how's it going?" Oliver greets me. In the background, I can hear the lively conversation in the coffee shop & deli that is Mindy's Place. It's a weird thing about Oliver. He has a perfectly good office upstairs that he could use, but he spends most of his creative time either in the basement taking up a corner of the metal table the pizza chefs use for rolling dough, or a seat in the shop if things aren't too busy. "You're quick on the call. You have an estimate for me already?"

"Hey, Oli, and yeah. How's the restaurant today?"

"Good," he says. "Mindy had the idea of running a panini lunch buffet, and she's got a line out the door. So the grill guys are going nuts. How's the house?"

"Man, how big is your bank account?" I ask, gulping down the sweet clean air of the backyard. It's a total mess too, but at least the smell isn't so bad. "Actually, check that. I know you could afford it. But if you want my best advice, get a couple of Molotov cocktails because this house needs to be burned down and rebuilt. It'd be faster and cheaper than trying to fix it."

"That bad, huh?"

A squeaking noise behind me reminds me of another thing, and I'm glad that I always wear some old military surplus combat boots when I go into places like this. "I'm not even joking about how bad this place is structurally.

And it's got rats, not mice, fucking Lower East Side sewer-size rats in the kitchen. You owe me for this one. I'm gonna need two showers to wash the stench off. And I'm thinking of burning this shirt."

I can hear the wheels whirring in his mind. It's what I respect about Oliver. Some people, they'd be pissed off that the house is so much worse than advertised. He isn't. He knows how to make a profit on this deal no matter what. "You up for lunch? If I smell another panini being grilled right now, I'm gonna lose it. Meet me at the taco stand over by the hotel in ten so we can stay outside. And I'll stay upwind of you."

I laugh. "Hey, at least you can see what a real man smells like instead of that fancy cologne shit Mindy has you wearing. But I'll take the tacos. See ya in ten."

Oliver laughs, and we hang up. Walking around the house to avoid upsetting the local rodents, I peel off my shirt and toss it into my tool carrier. I was serious about ditching the damn thing. I grab the bottle of antiseptic gel I keep in my glove box for emergencies and squirt my entire chest and arms. It'll dry out my skin some, but it'll at least cut the smell and make sure I don't get some funky ass fungal growth. I get my upper body as best I can before discreetly getting my balls and deciding that's enough. Pulling on my spare t-shirt, an old high school football shirt that's seen better days but still keeps a senti-mental place in my rotation, I drive over to the taco truck that's a mainstay in the downtown area near the Grand Waterways Hotel and Park. Oli's there a few minutes later, pulling up in his new car, a Lexus GX in silver gray.

"I see you're driving the soccer mom-mobile," I greet him, slapping hands with him. "What, Mindy's got the Ferrari?"

He's never had a Ferrari. He wouldn't blow his money on something like that, but he laughs. "Yeah, well, it's still stylin'. Come on, the tacos are on me."

The taco truck's famous around town for their fried shrimp tacos, and we get two each. Finding a spot on a nearby planter to sit down, I take a moment to inhale the aroma and to just enjoy the warm day. Now it's time to eat.

"So tell me about the place," Oliver says after we've both stuffed our faces. "I mean, I get your point. Firebombing the place would be easiest, but that's not exactly what I can put in an email without having the police knock on the door."

I fill Oliver in, and he winces. "Trust me, man, best thing to do would be to raze the place and start over. I'd bet even the foundation's screwed up."

"Okay," Oliver says casually. When I don't reply, he laughs. "Caleb, I know it's not because you're bullshitting me or being lazy. If you say it can't be renovated as is without being massively expensive, then that's what the deal is. Okay, it's settled. When I go back, I'll call the heavy equipment guys. You got another job lined up this afternoon?" Oliver asks, and I smirk. "Figured you were getting busy."

"It's not bad once you get past your mom's friends trying to get a little extra sugar to go with their repair work," I reply before telling him about Mrs. Barnes trying to seduce me with lemonade and cookies. "But other than that . . . business is booming."

Oliver chuckles. "Good, good, but what else you got going on, man? Every time we talk, you're about work. Rewiring this, tiling that, painting the other. What else is going on? You too busy working to get out?"

If there's anything about Oli that's a pain in the ass, it's his insistence on being a big brother to me. I get it. With Tony gone and Oli being a father now, he's got that instinct going strong in him, but damn, he can get a little nosy sometimes. "I literally just told you I'm getting propositions left and right, even with snacks! What about you and Mindy? Are the kids keeping y'all up all night still?"

Oli drops it. He can see I'm not in the mood, and besides, he can't pass up the chance to gush about the kids. "They're doing great, man. You gotta see them with their Grandma when she visits. It's pure comedy. It seems weird to think that we've got one starting preschool soon, though. Man, I'm telling you, you need to get one of your own. They're a hoot!"

Oliver stops, seeing the expression on my face, and I know he's seeing the warning flash in my eyes before he covers his faux pas with a smile. I let it go and give him a grin back. "Kids aren't in my future, or at least, no time soon. That's why I love to spoil yours rotten . . . and then send them back. I'm fun Uncle Caleb who lets them eat cake for breakfast, stay up all night, and jump on the couch!"

Oliver's eyebrows shoot to his forehead, and he half chokes on his *limonada* that we're having with our tacos. "You . . . let my kids eat cake for breakfast? Now I know why they came back last time begging to go spend the night at your place. Best keep that between us and not let Mindy know."

"What can I say? Your daughter gives me those big puppy dog eyes of hers and I can't do anything except turn on the cartoons and go get some cake."

Oliver laughs, nodding. "Yeah, she's good at that. Okay, we'll keep it between us because if Mindy finds out, you won't get a chance to babysit again, and I happen to like being able to take my wife out on the town every once in awhile. If you ever find a woman you want to marry, don't forget to do date nights. Keeps things solid, sane, and spicy."

"Sounds like a recipe for a good taco too," I wisecrack, and Oliver shakes his head. He knows I'm not listening, and he knows why.

"Okay, well thanks for checking on the house this morning. I'll have Martha get in touch with the heavy equipment contractors, see what we can get out there. As soon as I know, I'll get in touch with you on another property. Sure you won't do more scouting for me?"

I shake my head, offering him my hand. "No dice, Oliver. Besides, I heard Cassie's been doing well for you guys on that. She even skipped our run last weekend because she was, and I quote, 'gonna impress that man if it's the last

thing I do.' Apparently, you're *that man*. Lucky bastard."
I laugh.

Oliver nods. "Yeah, well, you should find the time for more than sharing a coffee downstairs. Seriously, both of you have momentum now. You can let off the gas a little bit and hang out for a change."

"You trying to play matchmaker with me?" I ask, and Oliver laughs. "What?"

"Caleb, I would be a horrible matchmaker. No, that's just general advice, and I know you two are friendly, that's all. Find the time when you can and hang out a bit. Be good for both of your mental health."

I think about it and nod. "If I find the time, sounds good. She's fun to joke with—you know how she is. Thousand and one laughs, and then I want to kill her."

"Yeah, I know someone just like that," Oliver says, meaning his wife, and I roll my eyes. "Anyway, take care, and don't eat too many of those cookies. You never know if one of my mom's friends has slipped something into the mix. You might find yourself tied up in someone's basement."

I laugh. "Sounds more like something Mindy or Roxy would do. Should I check your basement sometime for ropes, whips, and handcuffs?"

Oliver growls mockingly, shaking his head. "Think I gotta get back to work. See you later, Caleb."

CHAPTER 4

CASSIE

"*H*ey, Martha, it's Cassie," I say into my phone as I check that I've got everything I need. I'm quite the packer. Even going to the grocery store involves a packing list for me. And airports? The security guys there hate me with a passion. "Listen, I'll be out of the office today. I've got my eyes on three different properties that might be good purchases."

It's not a total lie. I do plan on spending most of the day working, but if I get done early, I still have some shoes to buy. I tell Martha a few details just in case she needs to get ahold of me, then I hang up and plug my phone into my dash dock where it'll work as my navigation if I need it. I'm terrible with driving directions. I don't think I could get myself from the office downstairs to the cafe if I didn't have it sometimes. Thankfully, I already input the three addresses for today's journey, and I check my other supplies. Laptop in case I need to send a serious email or something—check. Frappe from Mindy's Place for my morning caffeine buzz—check. Shoulder bag with my camera, wallet, and of course, all the other stuff I need to make sure I look good if I happen to run into Tom Hardy while I'm out—check. *Always gotta be prepared*. That's my motto.

I fire up my engine, and Roxy's cover of *Hallelujah* starts up. Damn, that girl can sing, and while she's not my entire playlist, it's a great way to start the morning. I cruise, letting my body relax as I get ready for a day in the 'mobile office'. I've always enjoyed this part of my job, working outside the office. Investigating new properties is fun. I always feel like I'm part *Sherlock Holmes*, part *Storage Wars*, and part *True Detective. House Hunters?* Please. I'm serious with this. I'm not going to be worrying if the kitchen has granite countertops or not. I'm looking for the deal.

It's probably the most fun part of my job. Most people, when they go looking for a house, they want the good stuff. They're looking for new carpets, fresh paint, all the bells and whistles. We're not. I want to find the worst house in the best part of town, pick it up at a steal, sink fifteen thousand into it, and either rent it out or flip it for twenty percent profit. In fact, the best way to get Steele Solutions to cut a check for your property is to make sure the carpet needs to be replaced.

It takes me about fifteen minutes to get to the first house, a two-bedroom for sale by a couple that's moving up and out. It's adorable and I love the all-brick construction, but as I get out of my car, I make sure to lock the doors. Our small town is nowhere near as bad as some of the nearby big cities, but every town's got 'that area', the part of town where the folks who just don't fit in live. Unfortunately for this couple, their house is right on the edge of 'the tracks', as we call it. On the edge, and looking around at the other houses, not in a good way either.

It's a shame too, because looking at the house itself, it'd be a place I'd love to live and start a family when the time's right. There's even a fireplace, and to me, nothing is more romantic than cuddling up in front of a real fire on a winter's night. But no amount of renovation to the house will make up for the decidedly unsafe street it resides on.

Hurrying back to my car, because Mama didn't raise no fool, I'm off to property two. Pulling up out front, I feel a little tingle of excitement. The house has got hidden appeal, as it's almost completely covered by a huge shaggy tree in the front that drapes down to meet the overgrown weeds standing as tall as I am. And while I'm on the shorter side, that's for a woman, not for a weed!

I get out of my car, checking my notes on my tablet before I try and fight my way through the jungle that is the yard. The house is in a good-ish neighborhood. It was just caught up in a court battle for years. An old man died, and his two sons fought over the family home. Finally, the probate court said fuck it, and the property's up for sale.

I walk up to the house, trying my best to keep to the cracked walkway. It's a shame, really. The two sons could have gotten a lot higher value for this place if they'd just agreed to split the sale or to just have one of them sell it. Fuck, flip a coin. Don't let a house get like this! Thank

God for jeans that make my ass look good and light hiking boots.

My initial excitement fades as I get inside. While the pictures that the website displayed showed the good side, they certainly hid the bad. All of the plumbing fixtures are corroded. The whole place will have to be repiped, and I bet from looking at the outlets, it'll have to be rewired too. I didn't think anyone even *had* outlets like that in their houses anymore.

As I make my way upstairs, I'm tallying a list of projects for the house, and even before I get to the spare bedroom that has no ceiling because a leaky roof collapsed inward, I realize it's not a money-making option. There's light damage that can be replaced and repaired economically, and then there are total renovations that cost more than they're worth. This house is definitely part of the second group. Damn it. Zero for two today. Off to the third on the list . . . and it's nearly an hour out of town, just over the county line.

I get on the Interstate and start to cruise. As I do, I realize that I'm not that far from the town where I lived as a little kid. I didn't always live near the big city. In fact, for the first ten years of my life, I was a country girl. I spent my summers swimming in the river, riding my bike like a crazy person, and camping in the backyard of what was the best house ever. Two stories, it was an old farmhouse that my parents had bought and renovated before I was born. While the farm itself wasn't ours, we still had a full acre to ourselves, a big garage, and a playset that gave me some of the best memories I could imagine. I haven't stopped by since moving back to work with Oliver. The memories are a little too painful to think about. Still, I'm pulled toward checking it out.

On a whim, I decide to get off the highway and head over to my old place. I haven't been back here in over fifteen years, not since my mom got a new job and we had to move, but the turns are familiar to me. The street curves. A few of the houses have changed, but I can still identify some of them.

When I see 614 Douglas, I'm slow driving, just sort of intending to do a drive-by of the old home. I'm certainly not intending to spend much more time than that. I have to get out to this third property for Oliver before the afternoon wears on any longer. But as I see the property, I hit my brakes, stunned. The house looks just like it did before, with the wide front and almost Alpine-steep roof that's broken up by two jutting outcroppings. I've always thought they looked like eyes over the long porch that wraps around the whole front. The railing is just like it always was, a sort of off-white that made me think the house was a smiling face.

But what causes me to smack my brakes isn't the house, but the sign out front. I blink, rubbing my eyes, but when I open them, it's still there, just like it was before.

For Sale by Owner.

Holy shit. My childhood home's for sale.

CHAPTER 5

CASSIE

I stare at the house from the curb, my brain swept away on a flood of memories, some good, some bad. Here, twenty feet away from me, is the oak tree that Mama didn't want me playing in, but I still did every chance I got since the trunk was split. She said it was because of storm damage when she was pregnant with me, but whatever the reason, thick branches started not that far off the ground, and to a little girl who loved to climb, it looked like a ladder to the sky. I scrambled up that ladder so often I knew every twist, nook, and cranny in the branches. At least, I thought I did until I was eight and slipped and fell. I'm lucky I got away with nothing but a small scar under my chin. In fact, it's still visible if you know where to look.

I step up onto the same sidewalk that I used to hopscotch down for hours, using chalk that I'd gotten from anywhere I could. I don't know why I was such a hopscotch nut. All of my friends outgrew the game by third grade, but I'd stay out until the streetlights came on and Mama would holler out at me from the kitchen that it was time to come inside for dinner. There's nothing drawn on it now, but to me, I can still see the ghostly outlines in pink, yellow, blue, and green and feel the bounce of my ponytail as I hopped along.

I shake my head—that girl hasn't been around for over a decade—and cross the yard. It needs some maintenance. The sign on the house is dusty, and clearly, the place has been up for sale for a while. Stepping closer, I can start to see why. While the rails on the porch have a relatively fresh coat of paint, the floorboards themselves are listing a little. I remember sometimes, right at the end before Mama and I moved, sneaking out to avoid the sounds coming from her bedroom as she and her latest boyfriend did things I didn't quite understand at the time. This was during the bad years, after Dad left, and Mama . . . well, she needed men like some people need water.

So I used to sneak out, sometimes to sleep in the tree-house I had in the backyard, sometimes just to walk around and smell the night air. I remember that the board just to the left of the window used to always squeak, no matter how hard we'd nail it down. Now, though, there's no way I'd trust myself to the porch. Half of the boards look dry rotted, and the whole thing is listing slightly to the back. Knowing my luck, if I take one step on that thing, I'd fall right through and end up with a splinter the size of a ballpoint pen in my ass.

I walk around the side, down the dirt driveway to the parking area in the back, what people in this area call a 'dooryard'. The garage is gone, just a concrete slab now, but other than that, little's changed. I can almost see Mama standing in the sagging screen door, calling my name. My eyes start to prickle with tears. I can almost feel a whisper of her there, but she's not. She's been gone for a couple of years now. While Dad and I are on polite terms, his life's not around here anymore. He probably hasn't been back here in twenty years.

But this . . . this is where I see Mama. It's in the buzz of the cicadas, the humidity, and the sunsets where the air hangs thick like sap around you. A place where your skin glistens five minutes after you dry off from the warmth, and every meal is accompanied by a glass of iced tea or lemonade just to get that cool kiss before diving into something spicy and most likely fried.

I check the back door. It's locked, of course, but the windows are just high enough that I can look around. The kitchen looks a mess, but the trained evaluator in me sees that it's surface mess.

Going around, I see the same thing repeated time after time. Most of the damage in the house is superficial, although there's some that's due to age. When I get to the corner room, where my old bedroom used to be, I know. This is my next project, the first one from find to finish, all mine.

I'll talk it over with Oliver, of course, mainly because I'll need the time to do all of this, but that's okay. I'm going to make this house all the things I wanted as a little girl. There were so many things that Mama said she'd fix but never did. The reason we could never fix anything was the same. "We don't have the money right now, honey," Mama would say, and while it was true, she spent more than enough money chasing after her boyfriends, usually on clothes to attract them or some other man.

But this house . . . I know what I need to do. Going around front, I take a few pictures of the property, then make sure I get the number on the *For Sale* sign down before I get in my car. I start up my engine and give 614 Douglas another look before pulling away. I've got one more house to look at for Oliver, and then I need to get home.

I've got research to do, and shopping for shoes online can wait.

CHAPTER 6

"*My name is Sue! HOW DO YOU DO?*" my radio blares as I pull up in front of Mindy's Place. Finally, after a few years of its being open, a lot of the people around town aren't calling it the Flaming Dragon building anymore, but the old nickname still sticks around.

Shutting off my truck's engine, I look inside, trying to decide whether I want to sit down and enjoy the atmosphere or if I want to grab 'n' go. It's not that I don't like the cafe, but at seven thirty in the morning, I'm in no mood to put up with pretentious bullshit, and sometimes, the local bankers like to turn Mindy's Place into Mini Wall Street. My jeans and work boots do *not* fit in with that crowd.

But they seem to still be asleep, and I remember that banks don't open until I'm already working today. I yawn, rubbing my eyes and feeling the intense need for caffeine. Getting out, I check my watch and decide I've got a few minutes to actually enjoy the cafe. Maybe I've even got time to enjoy a bagel. Not much more. I've got three jobs today, and unless I want to be roofing a garage by starlight, I need to get a move on.

Walking in, I see Mindy behind the counter, grinning a smile that's way too bright for this time in the morning. She must be sipping some of her own goods. I give her a wave as I walk up. "Hey, Beautiful, does your husband know you're here to see me every day?"

Mindy laughs. She and I have done this dance for at least the past year and a half, since I started helping out Oliver. "Pretty sure he knows you come in here to see me. In fact, he said if you stare at my ass anymore, he's gonna kick yours so hard you'll have a second crack. Steele lines it up . . . it's good!" she jokes, making a field goal sign with her arms.

I laugh. It's what I love about Mindy. Successful business owner, sure. But she's still approachable, and she knows I'm just messing around. Oliver does too, but I still gotta get my jabs in. "Any day he wants to try, but don't be sad when you have to take care of his broken body. I float like a butterfly, sting like a bee, and kick like a mule."

Mindy shivers and starts giving a phantom massage while gyrating her hips. "Do your worst, Caleb. I'll take care of my man's body anyway, anyhow, anytime."

I cringe and give up, laughing. "Ok, you win . . . I don't want a mental image of that. Ever. Can I get the usual?"

Mindy rolls her eyes. "For here or to go?"

"I have time to drink it here, but pack it to go anyway. And can you throw in a bagel with cream cheese? Gonna need the energy today."

"One of those days, huh?" Mindy asks, and I nod. She reaches down and pulls out 'my' cup, a fifty-ounce insulated cup with a built-in straw. Mindy twirls it on her finger and sets it down. "One Caleb-sized full-caff, sweet as my sister, roughly the thickness of motor oil coming right up."

I wander over to the far side of the counter and take a seat. It's my favorite. From here, I can watch everyone coming in and out of the door and still get to talk with the staff.

There's a rattle from the back, and I see Oli coming up the stairs from the basement kitchen. After a quick kiss on Mindy's cheek, he walks over, a mock scowl on his face.

"You here harassing my wife again?"

"Just for a minute. Gotta get my daily fix before heading out today."

He nods, taking the seat next to me. "Got anything interesting today?"

"Three jobs. The first two aren't much. Mrs. Henderson needs a bush yanked out of her yard—and no comments from you, Mindy. I realize I set myself up as soon as I said it!" I add offhandedly, getting a laugh from them both. "Then I'll do some painting for the Portnoys, and then the afternoon's going to be patching Kelly Roberts's garage roof."

Oliver nods. "You got time to go over a couple of things really quickly upstairs?"

"Yeah, of course, anything for you. You know that." The assistant who's been watching my coffee brings over my huge cup and bagel, which I pick up and make a quick sandwich of. I raise my cup to Mindy. "Thanks, Mindy!"

"Anytime, Number Three!" Mindy calls, and I have to laugh. It's a joke between the two of us. Oliver, of course, is Number One. I'm not even sure who Number Two is. But I'm Number Three on her list of guys. I'm good with that.

Following Oliver upstairs, I take a quick sip of my coffee, which they iced down just like I like in the summertime. I like hot coffee like any good handyman, but right now, it's damn near ninety degrees by ten in the morning, and I can use anything to cool me off.

Closing the door to save the cool air and give us some privacy, Oliver walks around to the other side, grabbing a stack of folders. "So I was thinking—" he begins, but stops. "Caleb, how backed out are you on your handyman stuff?"

"Right now?" I ask, pulling out my phone and checking my schedule. "If you're talking Monday to Friday, I'm booked through to next Thursday. If it's an emergency, I can bump people around, work on weekends. Why, what's up?"

"Nothing that's an emergency, but we just closed a few deals and I want to get them into rental shape before the summer's out," he said. "At least three of them are in the

University District, and you know that with the school year coming up . . ."

"You want them looking good for all the new tenants before classes start," I finish for him. "What're you looking at?"

"Two houses—nothing big—but also a sixplex that'll need a good amount of sprucing up," Oliver said. "I'm sure I could hire other people to go over them, but I trust you to do the job right and not fuck me over on hours either."

I nod, grateful for the straight talk. Oli's right, a lot of handymen and contractors around here charge guys like Oliver based not on how much the job's worth, but how much they think they can get away with. Not my style.

Oliver continues. "So what I was thinking, if you can, start the work on the sixplex as soon as possible, mainly just clearing the smell at first. You know how college kids are. Then move on from there. You're doing a roofing job today, so you've got a lot of the materials still, I take it?"

"Of course. What else?"

We go over the plans, and I'm glad to see that Oliver's right. Other than maybe jumping on the defunking of the sixplex, nothing is an immediate job.

"I think I can get this cleared out soon," I tell him and raise an eyebrow as he picks up another folder. "You must want to buy me a new truck."

"Not quite," Oliver says with a smirk. "This next one, we haven't made an offer on yet. I wanted to see if you can add a gable to the front to make it symmetrical. That one might need a drive-by and to check the codes."

"I can take a look on Sat—" I start, but before I can finish, the office door bangs open and Cassie comes in. Seeing her come into the office with her boundless energy lifts my mood. I never really admitted it before, but she's *stunning*.

She isn't dressed for success like she normally is, just in a t-shirt and jeans. What makes her stunning, though, is the light in her eyes, the fierce look of determination that I've seen before. When she's like this, the higher the Cassie volume is, the prettier she gets. And right now, she's cranked up all the way.

I'm looking at a five-foot-one hurricane of energy, moving so fiercely that I'm surprised her hair isn't flying out in all directions, her face lit up with a smile that could power Washington if it stretched just an inch wider.

"I found it!" she declares, jabbing a fist in the air. "I found the one!"

"The one what?" Oliver asks, amusement in his voice as I sit there, still too flabbergasted to talk. "And good morning, by the way."

"Yeah, yeah, good morning, guys," Cassie says before her sparkling eyes light up again. "I found my first project!"

CHAPTER 7

CASSIE

Slurping, I spoon the last of my Corn Pops into my mouth. I blink, wishing I had my morning coffee already, but I can't make coffee to save my damn life. At least, not compared to what Mindy makes, and it's like being exposed to real beef after eating nothing but tofu all your life—there just ain't no going back. I've tried bribing her to learn her secret, but she's not talking. So I only drink home brew if I'm in a pinch.

I was up all night last night looking at the property information on 614 Douglas, using all the websites I've got at my disposal for research. I did comparatives on the neighborhood, got in contact with the owner and got title information, pictures of the inside, and more.

By the time I lay down at four in the morning, I knew my initial feelings were right. The house is definitely going to be my first project. I just have to convince Oliver.

I still didn't get much sleep. The problem was, the

numbers just weren't golden. It isn't a shoe-in, as the comps really show that the profit margin is tight, at best, but I know I can do it. And more importantly, I *need* to do it. The house deserves it after surviving my wild youth. It's the home of some of my best memories, and it was the house that waited patiently while Mama and I kept promising to bring it back to its former glory . . . and we never delivered. I tossed and turned all night, mentally prepping my speech to get Oli to agree.

But I've only been working for Oliver for less than a year. Sure, I got the McCormick property off his back, but taking one albatross off only to put another one on isn't in his plans at all. But I've got faith. Still, I was so frenetic with energy, I had to resort to my trusty Mr. Rabbit because post-orgasm sleep is the best sleep. Even after the quickie session, though, I barely did much more than doze.

I get in my car and drive to the Flaming Dragon building, walking in the front door to see Mindy smiling and joking with the morning customers. The professional crowd is just starting to come in, and for the first time, I feel a bit out of place in the same jeans I wore yesterday. I was just so addled when my alarm went off that I was barely able to brush my teeth and pull on fresh undies and a decent t-shirt.

"Hey, Sexy Star," Mindy greets me, her normal big smile helping a little. She gives everyone in her 'family' nicknames, and I'm Sexy Star. I appreciate the gesture, really. "No offense, but you look like wired hell."

"Thanks," I reply, feeling a shot of adrenaline as I

remember why I'm here. "I've been up all night, so could I get a triple 'spresso with a shot of whatever you got that'll have me perky?"

"On it," Mindy says, grinning and heading over to the machine. "What had you up all night? New man?"

"Ha!" I say with a laugh. "No, I found something better. I found my first project. I need to talk with Oliver about it."

Mindy stops and gives me a warm look. "Good for you! If that's the case, I'll throw in some extra perkiness."

I slam my triple espresso, trying to build on the excitement and momentum that Mindy's words light inside me. Licking the last drops of dark, sweet liquid out of the glass, I take a deep breath and steel myself. "Okay, I'm off."

"Drop it like it's hot," Mindy says in farewell, and I chuckle, popping my hip into the door upstairs in reply. With every step up to the second floor, I can feel the excitement build in me, and by the time I reach the first landing, I'm almost running up the stairs. I hit the door, my prepared speech flying out the window as soon as I burst in, seeing Oliver at his desk.

"I found it!" I yell, fist pumping like a madwoman from the Jersey shore. "I found the one!"

"The one what?" Oliver asks, smirking. "And good morning, by the way."

"Yeah, yeah, good morning, guys," I reply, realizing that Caleb's there too. "I found my first project!"

"Your first project? Surely, some guy didn't ask you to

marry him since I saw you last?" Caleb jokes. "How much of a loser did he have to be that not only did he ask you, but you're calling him a *project* too?"

I stick out my tongue, blowing Caleb a raspberry. He's as handsome as ever, looking dressed for work, obviously, in his boots and t-shirt, with what looks like a nearly a pony keg of something in front of him on the desk, his personal drink holder that he takes coffee to work sites in. "No, smart ass. As if I want to get locked down into sandwich making for some dad bod who only surfs the couch. The house . . . I found *THE HOUSE.*"

It's pretty clear by the tone of voice I used that I'm saying it all in capital letters, and Oliver's eyebrows lift by a good half inch even as he leans back in his chair. "What house? Whatcha got?"

I take a deep breath and walk around Oliver's desk, opening up my bag to hand him a flash card and some of the stuff I printed out last night. "It's all on the sheet, but here's the basics. It's a three-bedroom converted farm-house on a quiet street, two and a half baths. It could become a four-bedroom, but one of the rooms has been used as a home office and walk-in closet. It's on a full acre of land, and there's a huge tree out front begging to have a tire swing on it, and a front porch. It's not quite a starter home. It's a step up from that, but it's the sort of home a young couple could raise a family in for the next twenty or thirty years if they wanted."

Caleb whistles softly. "Sounds idyllic. What's wrong with it?"

I glare at him. *Way to cockblock me there, buddy. I'm so going to take it out on you if I get the chance.* "Shush, I'm trying to create a mood here." I look back at Oli, who's giving me the same look, and I know I've got to get it together. I try to remember what the hell I was going to say with my speech and take a moment, opening my laptop and pulling up the pictures. "Here's the house. I know it's going to need some work—"

Oliver snorts as he scrolls through the shots. "Yeah, that's not the house you just described. Other than the obvious, what's it need?"

"It's a For Sale by Owner. I talked with the owner last night, and he was really helpful. He emailed me an inspection he got when he moved out. First things first, the porch will have to be totally replaced. Apparently, the guy tried to use trailer jacks on it and screwed up. The interior needs to be cosmetically gutted. The paint's at least eight years old, the kitchen lino over a decade."

"Looks like a refugee from the seventies," Caleb comments. "Lime green? Fuck, that's horrible."

"The whole place will need new flooring, but there's a hidden jewel underneath," I say. "I know for a fact that underneath the bad carpet in the rest of the house is real black walnut flooring. Sand it down and refinish it, and boom!"

"Black walnut flooring covered with carpet?" Oliver says wonderingly. "If it's still good, that could be helpful. Still, what are the costs involved?"

I give him a rundown of the costs, showing him the Excel

spreadsheet I worked up. Of course I don't have exact numbers, but it's a start. "Given the recent sale prices of properties in the area, I'd say the top price we could get on the sale is maybe three hundred thousand if we get an upswing in the area."

Oliver nods and looks over the spreadsheet some more before sitting back and tapping at his lip thoughtfully. "I'm going to be honest with you, Cassie. I admire the enthusiasm, and you know I appreciate your eye for visualizing what this house could be. And it could be beautiful. I see the outside of the house and I see what you mean. But look at the numbers. That's pretty tight profits. I'm not sure it's something I want to take on right now when we have higher-percentage investments on the books."

I shake my head, fire burning deep in my heart as I click back to the pictures. "I knew you'd be looking for higher-margin investments, and I have another we can talk later about too. But I can do this. I found it, researched it, and have outlined the project. I want to do it all, start to finish, and show you what I'm capable of. I obviously can't afford it on my own, but I do have enough for the down payment, so I'll have a stake in it. Just give me a chance, please?"

Caleb laughs lightly. "Think you're ready to fly solo, baby bird? I could push you out of the nest myself if you want." He gets up and reaches out with his long muscular arm to push me in the shoulder, but I hop to the side. He goes to follow but freezes when he sees the look in my eyes. "You're serious about this, aren't you? What's got you so fired up about this place in particular? By the time you get your profit, you'd probably have made more slinging frappes downstairs considering the number of hours it's going to require."

Oliver nods in agreement. "I don't think so, Cassie. You might be ready, and I'm willing to let you try. But it's not this project. Don't you want a sure thing your first time out?"

I shake my head, crossing my arms over my chest and putting on what I hope is my most stubborn look, although I've been told it looks pouty. I can't help it. I have a natural worry line that looks cute, dammit! "Nope, I want this one." I look from Oliver to Caleb and back, both of whom look less than impressed. "Look, it's *my* house. The one I grew up in. I want to fix it up, make it pretty and functional so it gets the family it always deserved. Right now, it's going to rot. I *need* to do this. I know that puts me starting off on the wrong foot. I know I'm using my emotions more than my brain on this, but that house deserves better than what's happening to it now. I'll put in work myself, elbow grease and sweat and blood and whatever else it needs. Please."

Oli looks at Caleb, who looks back. Both of them are definitely surprised by the vehemence in my voice. I know I'm sounding a little whacked over this, and yeah, I'm breaking rule number one of property investment, which is you make decisions with your calculator, not with your heart. I'm normally a perky upbeat smartass, so I'm sure this is a shock. But seeing 614 Douglas, I have to do this. Because there's more than just good memories there.

There are bad ones too, bad memories that aren't the house's fault, and I want to exorcise those demons from the house and from my soul. I want to sweep them away, leaving behind just the little seedling that's in the bottom of my heart.

Oliver looks at Caleb again, then at me. "Caleb? How much time can you clear over the next two months on your schedule?"

CHAPTER 8

CALEB

*A*t Oliver's question, I knew the inevitability of the situation. It was like watching fate at work. After Cassie's pleading, he had to give in. I got the call while I was at the Portnoys', cleaning up from painting their fence before heading over to the Roberts house to take care of her garage roof, where her son had somehow put a croquet ball through the roof.

Of course Oliver had his misgivings, he told me. He still made it clear that it was a risky investment, but he'd do it for her if she got it at the right price. And since I'm the handyman he trusts, he wants me to at least give her a heads-up on what all this place needs. So here I am, driving to meet her at her childhood home.

Normally, I'd be calling it a day and heading home by this point, two fat checks and a nice wad of cash in my pocket and nothing on my mind but grabbing a shower. Instead, I'm driving all the way into the next county to meet Cassie and the homeowner to do a quick walkthrough.

Pulling up, I can see the sun setting behind the house and it does look nice. Of course, that's probably because it's mostly in shadow and you can't see the porch hanging on by a thread that was readily obvious in the pictures this morning. Cassie's memories are seriously giving her rose-tinted goggles on this, I suspect, but I'll do my best to help her out.

I pull around back to the dooryard and see a backyard that's half jungle, half fire ant hill, and I cringe some more. The pecan trees are nice, though. I can see Cassie and an older man standing inside. Parking my truck, I walk to the door, carefully stepping over the suspicious-looking steps on the way up. It looks like more than the front porch will have to be replaced.

Opening the screen, I step inside. Cassie stops mid-sentence and stares at me, her mouth half hanging open in surprise. I realize that I might be a little unsightly after a day of work. I'm sure my hair is messy from running my fingers through it, my shirt has been wet then dried multiple times today—and it probably smells like a locker room—and my hands are still dirty from the roofing patch. Figuring I'd better start off on the right foot since she's with the owner, I hold my smartass comment about rendering her speechless and put an embarrassed smile on my face. Besides, he knows why I'm here. I don't need to be freshly shaven and wearing a suit.

"Hey, Cassie, sorry I'm late. Just finished up for the day and got here as fast as I could." To the man, who doesn't look that put-out at all, I give a respectful nod. "I'd offer my hand, sir, but you probably don't want it. I'm Caleb Strong. I contract with Steele Solutions."

Cassie still hasn't said a word, and I wonder for an instant if I've somehow offended her by showing up not smelling like Head & Shoulders. The man notices it, too, and breaks the silence. "Hello, I'm Frank Wannamaker. And don't worry, I've heard about you. I have a church friend who's mentioned you—Rebecca Miller?"

"Mrs. Miller?" I say, then smile. She's one of my favorite clients, friendly and professional with no funny business. The four days I was repairing her wall, I got lunch and ice cold tea almost every hour. "I hope her wall's doing well. Laying stone is an interesting challenge compared to brick."

Finally, after an awkward moment, Cassie shakes her head and returns to her speech. She's apparently discussing comp values and the sales price he's asking. I can quickly tell that Mr. Wannamaker is slightly overwhelmed but charmed at the same time. "Miss White, let's sit down," he finally says. "This wasn't really my house, but my brother's. When he decided to move down to Costa Rica to join some retirement community, I bought it off him to make sure he was taken care of. So I just want to get my money out of it."

Reassured that Cassie's got Frank well under control, I raise my voice. "Excuse me, Cassie. Do you mind if I look around a bit while y'all talk? Let me get an idea of what needs done?"

When she nods, I wander off, walking through to the

kitchen. I can still hear Cassie talking and laugh to myself. She's gonna get this house at a great price and he's not gonna know what hit him. She's in full-blown Cassie Charmer mode. Yeah, that's what she calls it when she's in the zone. She's mixing in giggles, little jokes, and business talk in this casual, overwhelming mix of hilarity that leaves people thinking she's an airhead. I saw her do the same thing when I helped her out when she first moved to town and took her car shopping. She ended up driving off the lot in a car that left the salesman looking slightly stunned, and I'm sure, upset later over how much he'd let Cassie get away with.

Somehow, though, she never makes people too mad at her about her charm. She's just too bubbly, nice, and supposedly airheaded to ever catch blame for it. I've teased her about it . . . multiple times, but damn if she's not good. She could sell ice to an Eskimo and he'd walk away feeling like he won. As I check out one of the smaller bedrooms, she walks in smiling from ear to ear. "Cass, I pulled up some of the carpet, and you're right, the floors can be refinished, but—"

"DONE!" Cassie says before starting to twirl and sing off-key. She's cute as hell, but she can't sing to save her life. "Cass gon' give it to ya—"

"What?" I interrupt her, throwing up my hands in a futile attempt at stopping her. "You already agreed on a price? Don't you want to know what the reno will cost or run it by Oliver first?"

Cassie doesn't stop her dancing, shaking her ass in a way that has me looking at her hips, but she stops singing at least. "Nope, doesn't matter. It's low enough that there's no way he'll turn it down. I told him I grew up here with my mama and I wanted to fix it up right. Showed him the corner of the fireplace where I chipped my front tooth and the faint little lines on the doorway to the kitchen where my height is marked. He said that was 'right nice' and agreed to my low-ball starting offer! Already gave me the keys and said we can finish the paperwork tomorrow, but he was good with a handshake offer!"

She continues her little celebration, grabbing my hands to try to make me dance. I'm not much of a dancer, at least not without having music, but I try my best, figuring if I don't, she's going to start singing again. And I can't have that. "Watch it, I'm still dirty from working all day. I'll get you dirty."

Cassie laughs, undeterred. "I don't care. Celebrate with me!"

"Figures you'd like to get a little dirty, wouldn't you? Just how dirty do you like it?" I reply with a raised eyebrow and a deep voice. But it's a joke, it's always a joke. This is what we've done from the first time we met. We make crude comments, double entendres, and tease each other mercilessly. It's been the cornerstone of our relationship. I don't think we've ever really said anything serious to each other, and when we have, I'm not sure if we're telling the truth or just joking again.

Cassie stops, her eyes gleaming in the dim overhead light, a seductive smile on her lips that has me feeling shaky. Maybe we've always joked, but right this minute, with that sultry look in her eyes, I wonder if I've been going about this all wrong. "You don't know the half of it. And my toys will never tell," she says cheekily. "They're sooo good to me."

The sudden image of Cassie playing with a sex toy sends another tingle through my body, and when I reply, my voice is huskier, deeper, more demanding. This time, though, I'm not joking, even if she is. "Toys? Oh, hell, you'll have to tell me those stories . . . slowly and in detail. Come on, I'll even buy you a celebratory dinner."

CHAPTER 9

CALEB

e walk outside and decide to take my truck to grab dinner. I open the door for her, because my mom raised me right, and then close her in before heading to the driver side. I open up, but as I do, the wind shifts, and I realize I've forgotten something. Reaching into my back bench, I grab my little 'clean bag' and unzip it. "At least let me put on a clean shirt."

"Great, I'm going to dinner with Sasquatch," Cassie jokes. "You know, I've got some perfume in my purse, if you want."

"Not in a million years," I say, reaching behind my neck and pulling my tee over my head. I use it to do a little wipe down over my abs and back, and then I do my pits last before grabbing a small bottle of hand sanitizer, rubbing it up my forearms and over my hands. I look up and realize that Cassie is staring at me, jaw hanging wide open. "See something you like?"

Cassie shakes herself, seemingly mentally and physically, and grabs my shirt, tossing it at my face. "You wish. Just daydreaming about the house. Now drive!"

I let her off the hook because she wasn't thinking about the house. She was thinking about me. I could see it in her eyes. It makes me smile, even if I know she doesn't really mean anything by it. We've been friends for a while now, to the point where we once went on a double date. That was a disaster, though, because my date instantly got jealous of my jokes with Cassie and didn't get that we just tease each other like that. But seriously, it's not a big deal. Slipping my clean shirt on, I throw the sweaty one at her as I climb into the truck. She squeals, as expected, and threatens to throw it out her window before tossing it behind her into the back.

"The usual?" I ask as I crank the engine. The music starts up, and Cassie nods in approval as *Disturbed* comes on. It's another thing that I like about Cassie. We both like a lot of different kinds of music so it's easy to find something we both enjoy. She can appreciate good rock, and I've even seen her humming along the few times she's heard country in my truck.

"As if there's any question. Now floor it. I'm getting hungry!" And with that, we head off to her favorite burger joint, a converted train boxcar with outdoor seating that's about halfway back to town called *The Little Diner That Could*. Cheesy name, and thankfully, even cheesier burgers. As we pull up out front, she clucks her tongue. "You realize it's been awhile since we've hit this place up?"

"You're the one burning the midnight oil on work stuff," I tease.

"And you're the one getting hit on by women old enough to be your mom with cookies and milk," she says, and I swear I'm going to kill Mindy or Oliver. How many other people know about my customers doing that?

"Actually, recently, it's been lemonade."

"Lemonade and chocolate chip cookies? Revolting!"

"Peanut butter," I protest, grimacing. Yeah, chocolate and lemonade are not a good mix at all. "Come on, let's eat."

I'm glad Cassie likes her burgers because I'm fucking starving. She can put away a burger almost as fast as I can. Her only bad habit is that she dips her fries in a chocolate milkshake. Disgusting, but it's her favorite so I just don't watch.

Walking into the diner, we grab our usual table in the corner where the breeze is at its strongest and wave at the waitress. A few minutes later, as we pick up our big, juicy burgers, I pause, holding it up like a drink. "And a toast— to Miss Cassie White . . . on a deal closed, on a project to be completed, on a first gig all to herself. You're gonna kill it!"

"And to my grunting caveman, whom I know I'm going to bug the shit out of as I get the place redone," Cassie says, raising her burger. We bump burgers in a slight mash of bacon, cheese, bread, and beef, but that's us. So what if it's not champagne? I ain't a champagne kinda guy. Burger toasts seem just about right for us.

"So, what do you think?" Cassie says before she takes a huge bite of her burger. She's somehow able to fit more food in her mouth than a girl her size should even attempt.

"Your manners are still horrible," I tease, taking advantage of the fact that she's got so much food in her mouth she can neither blow a raspberry nor stick her tongue out at me. "If you mean the house, I think I know some ways to shave a little off the repair bill."

"Really?" Cassie half mumbles before swallowing. "Caleb, I appreciate that, but I don't want to shortchange the house."

"It's not shortchanging," I say around a half mouthful of my own burger. "But there are still ways we can get better profits without hurting the renovations. I was thinking . . . you mentioned in your spiel this morning that the place will probably need new appliances, right?"

"Yeah," Cassie says, dipping a fry and noshing on it open-mouthed, smiling. If her lips weren't so damn cute, I'd be upset. As it is, I'm still disturbed. "What, you know a guy who knows a guy?"

"Actually, we both know the guy," I tell her. "I had to pull a water heater from one of Oliver's properties two weeks ago. Nothing wrong with the thing. It was brand new when the old owners sold the property, but it just wasn't big enough for a duplex. Oliver had me yank it, and I've got it at my place, waiting for the scrap guy. But . . ."

"Caleb, you keep this up and I'm gonna kiss you," Cassie

says before blushing. "I mean, I'll let you give me a back massage."

"Uh-huh," I say, hiding my surprise at her choice of words. "Oh, one thing, though, and this is non-negotiable."

"What's that?" Cassie asks warily, taking another bite of burger. "I'm glad to pay."

"No, not that. If I'm going to keep my other customers happy, Oliver happy, and somehow get that house done before you're ready to retire, it's going to mean working weekends. And not farting around for a few hours Saturday morning and then cutting out to go shopping type of work. I mean getting down and dirty for eight hours a day on weekends. But I want you there helping, either as my assistant or as my gopher."

"Gopher?" Cassie asks. "Hey, I'll have you know that the braces cured that very well!"

I shake my head, laughing. "That's not what I mean. I mean if there's something you can't really help me with, you can be ready to get me any tools I need."

Cassie nods. "I know what you meant. This is my first solo project, and I have money riding on this just like Oliver does. What do you think I'm going to do, sit at home while you do everything? But are you sure about working weekends? Don't you have plans?"

"Don't have much going on right now," I admit.

Cassie looks at me in surprise. "What about that brunette

you picked up at the grocery store? She looked very interested in you."

I laugh ruefully. "Susannah? We went out twice. Then she bought me a candle. Patchouli, with a picture of a kitten on the thing. Noped the fuck outta that quick, fast, and in a hurry."

Cassie bursts out laughing. "Over a candle? You ditched her over a candle? I mean, it's a pretty horrible idea for a candle, but to break up with her over it?"

I chuckle, shrugging. "It's a power move. She's trying to girly up my place so that when someone else comes over, she's marked her territory. I am not getting tied up like that."

"Not tied up like that, but how about other ways? I might have some pink fluffy handcuffs just your size. And I damn sure know how to use silk ropes," she says as she licks her straw. "You'd be sure to enjoy it."

I smirk. That's the Cassie I've come to know and appreciate. I just have to make sure I don't end up with milkshake on my head. Instead, I give her a wink. "Now that, I might consider. Depends on what you're gonna do if I were at your mercy?"

Cassie looks me in the eye with a glint of mischievousness and takes a long draw of her shake, hollowing her cheeks. She swallows with an audible gulp and then licks her lips to catch a tiny drop left in the center of her top lip. I can't help it. My eyes widen and I feel my cock swell in my jeans, and I know I'm in trouble. I mean, I've always known Cassie was cute, but now . . . goddammit, I'm in trouble if she's just joking.

Cassie waits just a beat and then speaks up "Game. Set. Match. Winner, Cassie White. And the crowd goes wild." She mimics a crowd cheering. Dammit, I should have known she was still being a wiseass.

CHAPTER 10

CASSIE

*A*s the water splashes over my shoulders, easing away the stress and excitement of the day, I sigh gratefully. I've always been a nighttime shower girl. Glad I'm not a man who needs to shave in the morning. I like being able to roll out of bed fifteen minutes before I have to go if need be. Not to mention, the warmth and massaging pulse of the water hitting me in that perfect spot between the base of my neck and my shoulder blades is one of the best ways to relax me enough to sleep. And other places, sometimes.

And boy, did I have a day that has me both keyed up and exhausted. I review the meeting with the homeowner in my head as I pick up my washcloth and start scrubbing down my body. It couldn't have gone better, and I don't think I could've gotten a better deal. As soon as I got the man's number on how much he paid his brother to take the property off his hands, I upped it by only ten percent, and he accepted. Even with that, I'm going to get the house for at least thirty percent under local market value.

It needs a lot of work, though, and I'm gonna need Caleb for most of the projects. I'll have to get him to block out his schedule for several weeks so that we can hit the market before summer ends. He's going to be a lifesaver, and 'Mr. Fix-It' could just be my ticket to turning this project into something that'll make me feel good and give me a little money to top it off. I know I teased him tonight —I always do—but I don't think I could do this without him.

As I think about Caleb, I flash back to when he walked into the house tonight. I know I gave him a little look about showing up like that, but holy fuck, he was walking sex on a stick. I know some women like clean-cut, suit-and-tie kinda guys, but not me. Give me the man who doesn't mind getting his hands dirty any day, his hair messed up from hard work and a day's worth of stubble shadowing his cheeks, and I'm just about ready to fall back and spread my legs. Add in smelling like he just spent the past eight hours busting his ass and is ready to spend some well-deserved downtime with his woman? Oh, fuck, yes.

When Caleb took his shirt off, I almost drooled down my chin. I know he works out a lot. Hell, we've gone for runs together most Sundays since I got on a health kick a while back. The healthy eating might not have stuck because *burgers are the angels' sustenance*, but the runs are awesome. But runs don't give you a damn eight-pack. Yes, eight. I know because I've counted them.

Twice.

Okay, maybe more. But the fact is, when I'm holding my sides and trying to keep myself from hurling because I've spent the past three miles trying to keep up with a guy easily a foot taller than me, and I need something to distract myself from the pain in my sides, Caleb's stomach is an easy target.

That's the way we've always been. I think it's an outgrowth of our first encounters as adversaries. What started out in open competition has transformed, and I like Caleb. But we've always teased each other mercilessly, and sometimes, even folks around us think we're a couple, but we've never taken it to that point. It's just the way we communicate, an evolution of the trash talking we used to do. Now, it's just sexy banter.

That doesn't stop the secret that I've kept hidden for the past couple of months, that deep down, I think Caleb is one of the sexiest guys I've ever seen. Caleb Strong sends my pussy into overdrive sometimes, and right now, I'm thinking that what Caleb doesn't know won't hurt him. With a grin, I start to move my hands over my body, tracing across my collarbones and down the outer edges of my breasts. I've always been a girl who loves her breasts played with, even if they're not big. A man who can give my breasts proper attention can make me melt like caramel.

Slowly circling toward my nipples, pretending it's Caleb's slightly calloused hands on me, I close my eyes and let the warm water add to my fantasy. I move my hands slowly, taking my time as my right hand plays with my nipples.

"Oh, God . . ." I moan, pulling on my nipples slowly, rolling them between my fingers and feeling the tingle rush down my body all the way to my toes. "Mmm, that's so good, Caleb. So good."

I stroke my other hand down my stomach, finding the wet curls at the top of my pussy. My fingernails scrape lightly over the soft hairs, down to my pussy, lightly cupping myself. I start rubbing, letting my fingers massage my soft outer lips, leaning back against the tiles of the shower as I slide a finger between.

"That's it, slide it in deep," I moan as I slip two fingers inside me. In my mind, I can see the steely tension of his forearm as he starts pumping his long, sensitive fingers in and out of me. The first things I noticed about Caleb— well, after his body—were his hands. They show such brute power, but I've seen his attention to detail and how graceful his calloused hands can be.

I roll my thumb, brushing it over my clit as in my mind, Caleb's abs flex like they did when he was reaching to grab his fresh shirt. I can almost smell the honest, manly scent of him. He's not one for body washes or exfoliating cleansers. Give Caleb Strong a bar of Irish Spring, and he'll come out looking and smelling like a god. My pussy throbs as my thumb works with my fingers, clenching and tightening, wishing it was him I was feeling. I take a deep breath, remembering how his shirt smelled like him —earthy, manly, with a hint of sawdust. Rubbing faster, I imagine him in little pink fluffy handcuffs and smile, but when I realize he's all mine to tease any way I want, I fall off the cliff into my orgasm before I even touch the imaginary him in my mind. "Oh, fuck," I moan as my pussy tightens around my fingers and my ass starts thumping into the tile of my shower. "Yes, that's it, Caleb, make your baby come."

The world gets swimmy, and after a moment where I might've actually blacked out, I return to the shower and finish washing up. This summer might be the best of my life. I'm going to get to spend hours a day with Caleb, getting all the eye candy I could ever dream of. I promise myself, as I pull my pajamas on and put on my hairband to get ready for bed, that I'm going to make the most of it, teasing him while getting plenty of footage for my internal pleasure memories. "I'm gonna make you hard enough you won't need a hammer to drive in any nails." I chuckle before yawning. "See you soon."

I'm asleep before my head even hits the pillow.

CHAPTER 11

CALEB

I sit in my truck, wiping my forehead with a towel as the air conditioner roars. I don't mind working up a sweat, it's part of my work, but damn if I don't enjoy the feeling of a strong blast of chilly air after I get done with the day.

Things weren't too bad today. Everything was relatively routine. I had to rewire a garage, dropping in a new garage door opener and putting in another outlet to allow a chest freezer to be installed. Thank God I didn't have to shove that fucker inside.

I reach for my phone, knowing I don't want to waste time, and dial Cassie. "Hello?" she answers.

"Hey, short stuff," I greet her, smiling as I lean back. "You ready to be my gopher?"

Cassie growls. She doesn't seem to like that word, which, of course, is why I'm using it. Still, she can't say much. "Yeah, I'm free soon. What's up?"

"Need you to swing by the house and go over a few ideas," I tell her. I've been by the house twice in the week since our celebration dinner, and Oliver told me to go ahead and roll on the repairs. But for all of his approval, it's Cassie's show on everything she wants to do . . . within reason. "I have a few ideas I want you to look at, especially the new kitchen and the color of the stain that you want me to use on the walnut flooring."

"So you've made all the choices then? This ain't your show," Cassie teases, and I run my fingers through my hair. Okay, so maybe I've gotten a little overzealous on it myself, but there's something about helping Cassie and this project that's exciting me a lot more than trimming someone's hydrangea bushes.

"Come on, Cass. You ready for this? We've got some work ahead of us, and I just want to be on top of things. You sure you can handle it?"

"And what if I want to be on top?" Cassie retorts. In my jeans, my cock twitches again. I can't help it. I don't know what it was about seeing her so excited in Oliver's office the morning she told us about the house, but it's like a switch has been thrown in my brain. I can't get her out of my head, and every tease she's giving me is running straight to my cock and making me want to push the line with her just a little further than normal.

Not that I can let her know I've been fantasizing about her nearly every night this past week. "When can you get there?"

"I was already planning on heading over. I'm changing

out of my work stuff. Ditching the skirt and blouse for jean shorts and a t-shirt. Keeping my sexy panties though."

Goddammit, now I've damn near got my cock hitting my steering wheel. "I'll be there in ten minutes. What about you?"

"Gimme twenty. I'll stop and grab some dinner. See you," Cassie says, the line going dead. I take a deep breath, trying to calm myself, but my cock is still determined to help me drive, so I shift around enough that I'm not going to cause an accident before putting my truck in gear and driving out to the house.

Douglas Street looks even more idyllic as I pull up, and 614 smells heavenly when I get out, inhaling the rich scent of the recently blooming flowers in the big unkempt acre of land out back. I take a moment and see the big empty chunk of concrete that used to be a garage, and while that would be a long-term project beyond what Cassie's got in mind for this flip, my brain starts making plans.

I've got enough time to change and wipe down a little before she pulls up, looking cute but also ready to work in a hip-hugging set of jeans shorts, hiking boots, and to top it off, a tied-off t-shirt that reads *Hello, my name is HOTTIE*.

"Got dinner for you!" Cassie greets me chirpily as she bounces over, my eyes glued to her tanned legs. Oh, I so need to get her. "Check it out!"

She holds up a plain brown box, setting it on the hood of

my truck. "So what's in the box?" I ask, and Cassie grins evilly, knowing what I'm talking about.

"What's in the box? What's in the baaaaaahx?" Cassie imitates, her voice nothing at all like Brad Pitt's but still effective, and I have to smile. She laughs before opening up the box. Chinese food.

"I say we check out the house first, and we can talk moo goo gai pan later," I reply, heading to the back door and opening up. "That is, if you can handle the bad news?"

"You'd be surprised what I can handle," Cassie says, sashaying past me and running her fingernails over my shirt. "Nice shirt. *Female Body Inspector*? I mean, really?"

Maybe I planned it, but I won't tell. "It's an old clean work shirt. All right, simmer down a notch. I can inspect you another time. I've got shit to show you, and it ain't my dick." We lock eyes, and there's a new tension, making me think maybe she does want me to whip it out. But then I see her eyes twinkle, and the moment passes, both of us breaking out in laughter.

Cassie rolls her eyes. "You won that round, but you've still got a lot of catching up to do. What do you need to show me?" she says, looking around the house, ready to get down to business.

"Might as well start in here," I say, leading her into the living room. "I started pulling up the carpet the other night—wanted to get a better idea on how bad the walnut floor was underneath—and while most of it's good . . ."

I show her the section that shares a wall with the downstairs bathroom, where water damage rings and warping are clearly evident. "This whole section will need to be replaced, which brings us to another problem."

"What?" Cassie says, squatting down. "The wood seems strong at least."

"Right up until the next rainstorm. That water is most likely from the bathroom pipes, which means I'll need to totally redo the bathroom—walls, floors, all of it. It'll take some work getting everything to look right if we're sticking with hardwoods."

"You can handle it, right?" Cassie asks, turning around. She looks up at me with her big hazel eyes, biting her lip. "I do love the idea of the hardwood floors."

I swallow back my first thoughts about what her eyes are making me think of and nod. "Yes, but the stain would have to be carefully selected to make sure it blends the old and the new wood. We'll have to sand the whole floor anyway, but that means a lot of time on your hands and knees with a sandpaper block to get the edges."

"Time on my hands and knees, huh?" Cassie asks, reassured, her sauciness coming back. "I bet you'd like that."

"Yeah, well, it gets worse," I say, ignoring her comment even as my cock doesn't. "The kitchen needs to be gutted — floors, cabinets, counters, the works. But first, I need to show you something back here in the bedroom."

I head for the stairs, intentionally skipping the second, which creaks, and I'm going to have to replace it. I can't stand creaky steps. They remind me of haunted houses or something.

Cassie chuckles. "Is that how you get all the ladies to your bedroom?"

I look back over my shoulder, where I swear Cassie's looking at my ass. It makes me smirk. "No, I'm more caveman than that. I just grunt. Woman. Bed. Now." I growl, intentionally lowering my voice more. "And they tend to run that way."

"Hmm. I can see how that might work on some women. Especially the ones you gravitate toward. That's probably all they can understand. Complete sentences are just a little beyond their capabilities, aren't they?" She's joking, a little, but if I'm honest, I'm not usually looking for a brilliant conversationalist in the women I see.

We walk into the bedroom, and Cassie stares at the ladder extending up into the ceiling. "Uh, I don't think that was there before. Why is there a new hole in my ceiling?"

"Joke about your holes later, but if you look, there's a water spot on the ceiling. Yeah, a wet hole," I reply with a wink. "I uh . . . *probed* it to see how wet it was, and the ceiling panel just crumbled away. Climb up and see for yourself. The joists are water damaged too."

I gesture at the ladder, and Cassie carefully climbs up as I hold it steady. It's hard, but the ladder literally puts her ass right in my face, and my mind floods with images of me bringing my head forward, grabbing her hips, and seeing what my tongue can find. Still, I keep my composure as her head disappears into the hole. Knowing my voice is probably already husky with desire, I clear my throat before telling her, "Look to the right. The cross beam is there."

"Can't see much. It's pretty dark," she complains.

"Here," I reply, passing up my little penlight I keep on my keychain. She shines it around, and I hear her curse under her breath.

"Is it the roof?" Cassie asks, her voice still muffled. "I don't see any water there."

"No, the roof's good. I got up there and checked that," I tell her. "I'm guessing they fixed it but didn't check here."

Her ass has been wiggling back and forth in front of my face as she tries to see the various areas of damage. I can't help it. The hypnotic sway has me mesmerized, and my voice sort of catches in my throat. "Caleb?"

"Huh?" I ask as Cassie peeks back down through the hole and catches me red-handed.

"If you watch closely enough, it'll do tricks." She sways her hips back and forth again and then sticks it out, popping it a little like she's on the dance floor. I watch her little show, enthralled by her before shaking off the effect she's having on me. I laugh and give her a good smack on her right cheek. She lets out a cry of shock, rubbing her ass. "You did not just do that!"

"Yes, I did. You deserved it. Get down here or I'll do it to the other side so you have matching handprints."

Cassie climbs down, turning when she's halfway down so

that she can look me directly in the eyes, her voice dripping honey and her eyes twinkling. "Is that a promise or a threat? I can't tell."

I pause, uncertain of how to respond. My cock knows what it wants, but I'm a little worried about crossing a line that, once we cross it, can't be uncrossed. Still, she looks so hot in her outfit there on the ladder that I'm fighting the urge to pull her toward me, to grab her ass in my hands and see how far I can go. Finally, I swallow and step back, helping her off the ladder. "Come on, let's eat the Chinese before it gets cold. And then we've got an errand to run."

CHAPTER 12

CASSIE

I tuck the last of my eggroll in my mouth, trying my best to hide my frustration, but finally, as Caleb pulls into a parking spot and shuts off the engine, I can't help it anymore. "Really, Home Depot? It's Friday night and we're at Home Depot. We might very well be failures of the human race."

"Failures?" Caleb asks, chuckling. "You're getting what you need to grab your slice of the American dream, and doing it with your own two hands. What could be better than that?"

"Yeah, yeah," I grumble. "You're right."

Caleb chuckles. "I know I am. Now come on, let's grab some wood." We get out of the truck, Caleb coming around to make sure I can get down from my seat. "Then maybe later, you can grab mine?"

I chuckle. That's the Caleb I want to hear and enjoy hanging out with. Things have been feeling a little different lately. And honestly, my mind has been running a fantasy reel in my thoughts, mostly involving Caleb, that t-shirt, and not much else. "I don't know. I have a date later. Bob might object."

Caleb stops and looks at me, and I swear I see a hint of jealousy. "You have a date? Who's Bob? You haven't mentioned him."

I stammer for a moment. "Uh, no, I don't have a date. It was a joke."

"Then who's Bob?"

I raise my hands defensively, trying not to laugh that I've gotten another one over on Caleb. "Nobody, it's just an expression."

"Don't make me Google it . . . who's Bob?" Caleb growls intensely. The look in his eyes . . . I'm starting to wonder.

I can't hold it back anymore. I start laughing hard. "It's an acronym. B-O-B. Battery Operated Boyfriend." I can see the realization dawn on his face, and then he lights up in a big ol' shit-eating grin.

"Hot damn, woman, that's a show I'd pay money to see. What time's your date?" he asks, playing along now. I blush and give him a little push, feeling his pecs under my palms, but he doesn't move. He's steady as a statue. He smiles and then grabs my hand, almost dragging me toward the lumber aisle.

"Come on, I wouldn't want to keep you from your very important date," he says as he grabs a few 2 x 4s, placing them on a flatbed dolly. I stand motionless, watching the swell of his arms and shoulders as he picks up the heavy beams like they weigh nothing and noticing the little strip of skin that shows as his shirt rides up. He stands with his hands on his hips for a moment, obviously lost in thought. "Can you stay here with the cart for a minute? I need some screws from a couple of aisles back. I'll be just a sec."

He walks off with a determined stride, and I find myself alone before I can even reply. I cross my arms, huffing and waiting. "Fine then, I'll just entertain myself!" I call after him, but he doesn't turn around.

I stand there for fewer than ten seconds before a guy in an orange apron comes up, a smile on his face that looks like more than just friendly customer service. I swear, I see him look me up and down before meeting my eyes. "Hey there! Can I help you with something?"

"No, thank you. Just waiting for my friend to come back," I say, but it doesn't seem like that's enough to deter him.

"I'm John. Doing some house work?"

I smirk. This guy's probably thinking that I'm over my head and that I don't know a claw hammer from a screwdriver. "A ceiling repair project. We have to repair some joists before putting the new ceiling up."

"Wow," John says. "The 2 x 4s are good for that, but have you considered using 2 x 6s? They distribute . . ." He continues to talk to me, obviously trying to chat me up, and while he's cute, he's not my type. But he gets an 'A' for effort in trying to be sly about it.

A few moments later, Caleb comes stalking down the

aisle, his face stony. He walks up to me and puts his arm around my shoulders, pulling me close to him. I fit just under his arm, my head right at his chest level like we're a perfect match. "Hey, babe. Can't leave you anywhere, can I?" he says, and I can't reply. The feeling of his arm on my shoulder and the undeniable aura of his body being so close to me has me stunned. "I found those screws, and I see you've found a friend."

"Ah, yeah," I mutter, unable to pull myself away from him. I don't want to either. "This is . . ."

"John," Caleb says, staring him down for a beat after glancing at his nametag. "Thanks for the help. I've got this handled. Appreciate your expertise." I can't help but notice the hint of sarcasm to his tone.

Before John can say anything, Caleb lets go of me and grabs the dolly, pushing it with one hand and interlocking his fingers on the other with mine. Paying quickly, we get outside, load up the truck, and climb in. As soon as he starts the truck, I turn in the seat, bringing a knee up to my chest. "What was that about?"

Caleb looks at me for a second, then shakes his head. "Sorry, Cass. I shouldn't have jumped in like that, but he was obviously flirting with you."

I bite back a smartass reply, mainly because my body is still tingling from his putting his arm around me, and my hand feels like a low-grade fever's running through it where our fingers were entwined. "Uh, yeah. I'm aware. But it's not like he asked for my number or something."

His face twists a little, like he just swallowed something nasty. "Would you have given him your number?"

I shrug, forcing my knee down to turn and look out the front window of his truck. "I don't know. Maybe. It's not like I've got guys lining up to date me. You know how it is. I'm still the new girl in town, and I work for a guy who's intimidating, to say the least. And I've been putting my head down and busting my ass to get started on the right foot. It seems like most of the guys around here want a girl who's happy with dinner and dancing, maybe a little Netflix and chill."

Caleb snorts dismissively. "You're better than that, Cassie. Don't do that to yourself. That young stud in a fucking apron isn't your Mr. Right."

"You're probably right, but maybe I don't even want a Mr. Right. Maybe I just need a Mr. Right Now," I say, raising my voice. He's got some nerve. He's not the one who sees almost all the good options snatched up, except for the one who's put me firmly in the friend zone. "Don't get high and mighty on me, Caleb. I know you've done the whole one-night stand thing before, so don't give me any shit."

"I—" Caleb starts before snapping his jaw shut, the muscles clenching. I watch the muscles in his forearms and jaw twitch as he drives me home. We'd decided it would save time tomorrow if I just caught a ride with him. The whole time, he doesn't say a word, his eyes glittering with suppressed anger instead.

We pull up in front of my apartment building, and I look

over at him, waiting for something. Instead, he hits the button on his console and my door unlocks.

"I'll see you bright and early. We've got work to do," he says quietly, and I realize I've been dismissed. I climb out, closing the door and stepping back.

"Caleb—" I start, but before I can say anything, he's pulling away, my new 2 x 4s sticking out the back of his truck, the safety rag flapping merrily in the wind as he disappears into the darkness. I stare after him, unsure of what just happened. I mean, we've argued before, sure, but mainly about things that were forgotten a few minutes later.

But this was just weird . . .

CHAPTER 13

CALEB

uming, I drive the last screw on the reinforcement into the crossbeam, taking a look at my work. It was a pain in the ass bringing the beams up the ladder to the crawlspace, but it's done, and I check them one last time. Everything looks good.

"If only *she* were here to see it," I mutter, climbing down through the hole I've torn in the ceiling. I can get to that next weekend. I already rearranged my schedule to have this Monday to work here, hoping to get a jump on things. Looking around, I feel tired, more tired than I thought I would be. It's been a few days since I've seen Cassie after our fight. She skipped out on helping out at the house for the past two days with some pretty lame excuses. The thing is, I'm not really angry at her, although I'll admit I've muttered a few curses as I've struggled with a few things that an extra set of hands would've come in handy with.

Friday night, I went home, riled up and not really sure

why. I've never reacted to Cassie's flirting with some dude that way. Hell, I've even introduced her to a few. But that guy was slimy and didn't deserve her.

"Bullshit," I mutter, chastising myself. "Great, now I'm talking to myself too. Cassie is officially driving me crazy." But I can't stop. No, if I'm honest with myself, he wasn't slimy and was just talking to her. I just didn't like it. And now she hasn't even stopped by her house to check on the progress. Her car's still parked in the dooryard, even.

It's obvious she's avoiding me. Yeah, she might be busy, but she said she wanted to be involved every step of the way. I need to apologize, but fuck, I don't even know how to start.

I don't fully understand *why* I reacted to that guy the way I did. It can't just be that Cassie and I were flirting in the parking lot. Hell, we've done that for over a year, and the closest we've ever gotten to moving past jokes and flirting was our runs together. I mean, I've seen guys literally *grind* on Cassie sometimes when we've gone out playing wingman for each other, and I didn't bat an eye.

I'm gonna have to suck it up and act like an adult, though, because I need to go over tile choices for the bathrooms with Cassie. They have to be ordered and there's a few weeks' lead time to get them in, so I've got to talk to her . . . tonight. Whether her not showing up is through my fault or hers—and yeah, it's mostly mine—I have to heal this rift.

Running my fingers through my hair, I dial her number

and listen to the rings, not sure if I'm hoping for voice-mail or for her to answer. When I get the recording, I'm disappointed . . . guess that answers that. I leave a stammering message. "Hey, Cass. I, uh . . . need you to make some decisions so I can, uh . . . order supplies. Can you swing by tonight on your way home? Or, shit, I just remembered your car's still here. Gimme a call and I'll come get you. I'll be here 'till six thirty or so. Yeah, so . . . see ya." I hang up, shaking my head. "You are such a fucking dumbass, Caleb. Swing by, when her car's out back. Why not just hit yourself in the head with your hammer? Or better yet, smack yourself in the dick. You're thinking with it too much."

It's true. For the past few days, I can't get my mind off Cassie. Maybe it's that I've spent a lot of time in her house, but it feels like more than that. From the moment I saw her come into Oliver's office that morning, it's been like a switch was thrown in my head. She's more than just a cool girl, the girl I can throw taunts and jokes at without worrying about being taken the wrong way. Now . . . fuck it, I *want* her. Not as a friend, not as a jogging buddy.

I want to *have* Cassie. I want to feel her ass in my hands, to run my lips along the curve of her neck, to feel her wrap her body around my cock and make her moan and squeal as I send shockwaves through her body. I've thought about fucking her in passing before, but now I crave it.

Whatever. It's not gonna happen. If it were, it would have long before now. Besides, I've got shit to do today. I don't have time to worry about some damn crush or whatever this is. So back to work. After I cut the supports over the master bedroom, I delayed on the installation, hoping that Cassie could be here to help me out. Instead, I've focused mostly on demo the last few days, making the house look like a shell inside. There are walls with no drywall, just the studs allowing you to see from one room to the next. And today is kitchen day. It's a full gut job too, but I'm going to try to save the cabinets to donate. They're not in bad shape, just dated, and they don't work for the open floor plan Cassie has in mind. Saving might be the right thing to do, but it's not the fast way.

I almost wish I could just roll in and swing my sledge-hammer and knock some shit around. Flat-out mindless destruction always does wonders for the mood. The high after going apeshit on an old brick wall or fence is nearly godlike. Giving it a thought for a moment, I know I'm not doing that. Cassie'd be mad, and I'd be mad at myself later. With a big sigh, I head into the kitchen, turn on some tunes on my portable boom box, and get started. Hopefully, I can have it all empty before Cassie comes by tonight . . . if she does.

I get the stove and water heater outside using my dolly, loading them into the trailer that I'm using to haul stuff to the scrapyard. But working alone is hard, even with a heavy-duty dolly. I have to muscle both of them inside the trailer, and it takes up a chunk of time. By the time I'm done, I'm covered in sweat again, and I peel off my shirt, wishing that the water were on in the house. I could really use a hosedown right now, but all I've got is about a gallon and a half of unsweetened tea in a cooler. Instead, I use a towel to wipe down and go back inside.

I start carefully unscrewing the cabinets from the walls, carrying them one by one out to the curb for the donation truck to grab them later this week. It's finicky work. Some of the cabinets are long, and it takes time to make sure I don't just tear an anchor out of the wall, damaging either a cabinet or the support post behind it.

Still, I make progress, and hours later, the kitchen is well on its way to being stripped. I'm squatted down, head under the sink, unscrewing the drain pipes so I can remove the last section of cabinets, when I hear a loud noise behind me. The unexpected sound makes me jump, and before I can stop myself, the bottom of my head smacks into the sink with a resounding *BONG!* that leaves me seeing stars. There's a faint taste of blood in my mouth where I bit my lip.

I hear unsuccessfully suppressed giggles even as stars swim in front of my eyes, and I know who it is. I ease my way out from under the cabinet, holding the back of my head. "Holy fuck, Cass, you scared the shit out of me!"

She laughs, crossing her arms over her chest. She's still in her work clothes, looking sleek and professional in her white silk blouse and slim burgundy slacks. Her sky-high heels add several inches to her tiny frame, bringing her face even closer to mine. As I peruse her body, I wonder for a moment how she got out here. "You deserved it for listening to *Bon Jovi* while you're working. How old are you? Need me to get you a cane, Grandpa?"

"One, *Bon Jovi* is timeless and whips the shit out of half the acts out there today. Two, eighties rock fits right into my mood when I'm working like this, so get used to it.

Besides, we're close enough that we could have gone to high school together. So I'm more than young enough to throw you over my knee, brat."

Cassie chuckles, and I hope for a moment that everything might just go back to normal, avoiding whatever awkwardness we had the other night. "Yeah, well, you've got an old soul then, Caleb. Where'd you leave your steel horse, cowboy?"

I laugh. "See, I knew you liked *Bon Jovi*. You probably know every word to the song you're making fun of me for listening to." I pause, seeing if she'll agree or disagree, but she just sticks her tongue out at me. "How'd you get here anyway?"

"Oliver's babysitter, Emily, gave me a ride. Her best friend lives out this way, so she didn't mind. And I need to get my damn car anyway."

I know Emily. She's a nice girl, just a little shy. She's apparently great with Oliver's kids, though, and I think she's just the kind that takes a while to relax enough to get to know. "Okay, well in the meantime, come here and help me, woman. I'm taking out the sink to get this last bit demo'd for the day." Climbing back under the sink, I get back to work disconnecting the drain pipes, capping them off for later. I clamp off the feed hoses and disconnect them, making sure the hoses are clear before tapping on the bottom of the sink.

With a little bit of wedging, we slide our fingers underneath and pull the sink out. Once we get it out, I take the other end from Cassie and carry it outside to my trailer.

When I come back, she's leaning over the hole in the countertop, looking at all I've done. "Wow, you know, I was thinking, and I'd like to—"

As Cassie talks, she taps the clamp that I've put on the cold water line, and it pops off, the hose popping free to squirt both of us from the chest up in cold water.

"Oh!" Cassie yells, wiping at her eyes. "Shit, what the—"

"Damn it," I say, trying not to laugh. I reach down, and with blurry vision, I grab the pinch clamp from the floor by my left boot. I attach the clamp and then check the other.

"What just happened? Isn't the water off, Mr. Fix-It?"

"Yes, the water is off, but there's always a little left in the lines. The water company just shuts it off at the street and leaves it to the homeowner to bleed the pipes. Obviously, they didn't here, and with the heat . . . guess the pressure was just enough to blow when you tapped the cap. Pun intended." I finish my check. It'll hold. "Anyway, that should be the worst and—"

I turn around, seeing Cassie, her shirt clinging to her body and her hair in wild disarray as she shakes it free, and time stops. The words instantly die in my throat, and the only thought I have is simple.

I fucking want her.

CHAPTER 14

CASSIE

*M*y hair's a mess, and the blouse I wore to work today is soaked as I wipe the water out of my eyes. Caleb makes a joke, but I don't hear it as I'm trying to get a drop of water out of my ear, and I've got a finger jammed almost painfully in it. Finally, I pull it out with an audible *Pop!* just as Caleb stands up. "Anyway, that should be the worst and—"

He turns around and freezes, our eyes locking. Time seems to stop outside. There's some sort of weird magic going on. I'm not sure what he's thinking, but I'm looking at the rivulet of water running from the lock of wet hair lying over his forehead. The drop continues down his cheek, getting absorbed into his beard scruff, and all I can think is that I would've liked to lick that drop, catch it with my tongue, and suddenly, I'm *thirsty*.

He's staring at me too, towering over me, barely a half-step away. Even wet, I can feel the heat coming off his body. He reaches up, gently grasping a lock of my hair, tucking it behind my ear, and I wonder vacantly if he wants to lick the water from my face. I shudder a little at the thought, bringing his attention lower. He stares at my wet blouse, clinging tightly to my breasts. I look a little like a wet t-shirt contestant, my white blouse sheer and showing the lace of my bra. Can he see the pink of my nipples? I should probably be embarrassed by that, but instead, I find myself arching a little, hoping that he can.

He notices. I can tell because I see his eyes dilate, his breath coming faster. For a frozen moment, I think he's going to make a move, and I realize that I want him more than I have ever wanted anyone before. Wait, what? We're supposed to be friend-zoned buddies, that platonic friend that we tease but don't cross a certain line.

That might have been the past, and we've tap-danced that line plenty of times before, but right now, I want Caleb to make a move. As my brain whirls from the thoughts rushing through it, he sets his hands on my waist. "Caleb . . ." I whisper, my throat catching as the words get stuck somewhere in the back of my throat.

He takes it as a rejection, though, and the light in his eyes dims some, but they still burn with an intensity that leaves me breathless and my body aching for his touch. He gently pushes me away and growls in a gravelly voice I've never heard from him before, taking a shuddering breath. "Sorry, Cass. I got a little struck for a moment. It's been a while, and you do know how to render a man stupid."

I can tell he's trying to reset us back to the flirty lightness that is our usual mode of chatter. A little struck myself, I smile and step back. "All good. Listen, I know I was stupid over the weekend. It's my bad. So come into the living room. I brought pizza and beer for dinner." I start to walk out of the kitchen, noticing with a flutter that Caleb adjusts his crotch before following me. I've spread out a drop cloth I found in the entryway along with the six-pack and the two pizzas, Hawaiian for me and extra meat and cheese for him. "What do you think?"

Caleb's voice still sounds gravelly. There's still an intensity to it as he settles down, but he cracks a smile that leaves me fluttery inside. "Great. I'm starving. And about Friday night—"

"Forget it, let's dig in," I interrupt him, not willing to get into it. I don't want to tell him how, while I was taken aback at first, over the weekend, I didn't come to the house because I understood, and I felt like an idiot for flirting with the guy at Home Depot. If you could even call it that. When I think about it, there was nothing more that I wanted to do Friday night than spend the whole time with Caleb. I just don't know how to say it. Instead, I pop the top on two beers, handing him one. "Cheers. Sam Adams to the rescue."

We inhale the first few slices and couple of beers, relaxing as we talk about house stuff. He fills me in on everything, and I'm impressed with the amount of work he's done in such a short time. I also like the way he wants my opinion on things, not just because it's *my* house, but because he knows I have experience and ideas and he respects that. In return, when he tells me that I can't salvage the electrical appliances to save money, I trust him. Even if he does make a joke about my being shocking enough that I don't need actual electric sparks, too. We start to get a little buzzed, not impaired, but just enough to lower our inhibitions. After looking at me for a moment, Caleb sets his beer down and steers the conversation back toward us again.

"Hey, Cass, I'm really sorry about the other day. It just bugged me for some reason. You deserve a guy who's gonna treat you right, be your Mr. Right, not some stand-in. But what you do is your business, and you're right, I'm in no position to judge because I'm not a relationship guy either, at least not anymore. Been there, done that, got the *Fuck You* t-shirt, and ain't doing that again. I can't fault you for not wanting to deal with that either."

Maybe it's the beer, maybe it's just that we've spent almost an hour hanging out like we do, even if I still look at him and want to rip his clothes off. But I've never heard about this, and I feel more comfortable. I'm intrigued. "Apology accepted. You wanna talk about that t-shirt?"

Caleb snorts. Maybe he's slightly buzzed too, shaking his head. "Fuck, no. I got screwed over pretty badly, so I'll pass on a stroll down memory lane, chapter Wendy Reinhart. You wanna talk about why you want a Mr. Right Now instead of Mr. Right?"

Wendy Reinhart? The name rings a faint bell, but right now, I don't care. Instead, I think about right now and what I want. Right. Now. "Nope," I reply, emphasizing the word with a pop. I give him a look, scanning up and down his body, with a stop on his crotch. "That's a really BIG issue."

Caleb squirms a little, and I swear I see another big issue growing in the crotch of his jeans. "Uh, Earth to Cassie . . . my eyes are up here," he says, waving in front of his crotch to stop my eye-fuck.

I must be more buzzed than I realize, because before I know it, I'm grinning and letting my mouth and libido do the talking. "I have an idea. Hear me out."

"Do I want to hear it? Considering how you were just staring at my junk."

That's anything but junk, buddy. "You're not a relationship guy. I'm not a relationship girl. We're friends. And if we're both honest, there's some chemistry or we wouldn't be able to joke around the way we do. Right?"

"Uh, yeah . . ." Caleb says, obviously uncertain about where this is going.

I bite my lip, giving him my cutest, most seductive look. "I'm just saying, instead of rolling the dice on some asshole we meet at Home Depot or wherever, we should take care of each other! It's perfect. No strings attached, no commitment, no hard feelings. Just casual hookups and we can still be friends."

Caleb shakes his head, then looks hard at his beer, probably trying to figure out whether he's totally wasted or not. But he's only on his second can, same as me. Finally, he looks back, wonder on his face. "Cass, I'm damn near sure I misheard, but . . . are you asking me to be your fuck buddy?"

I grin, nodding. "Yeah. Buddy. Fuck. Let's be fuck buddies.

You in? Pun intended." I move closer, taking his beer out of his hands and climbing into his lap. My blouse is mostly dry now, but I still straddle his jeans, looking into his eyes as I press my body into his. "Caleb, you're the one guy in the world I trust with this, but it's your call. What do you say?"

For a heartstopping moment, I think he's going to push me off his lap, play off what I'm saying as just another joke in the infinite line of teases and taunts we've leveled at each other. Hell, he's probably waiting for me to say *GOTCHA!* I'm just about ready to play it off myself when he reaches around, grabbing my ass and squeezing.

"Fuck, yes, I'm in," he growls in that same deep voice that has my pussy aching before covering my mouth with his own. It's heady, intense, and I can feel the stubble on his chin and cheek rasping against me, fiery tingles filling my brain and making me wet again. Caleb's strong hands squeeze my ass, and his tongue urges my lips apart, demanding entrance.

I happily give in, and our tongues tangle, twisting as I tug on his hair, wiggling my hips over the swelling bulge in the crotch of his jeans. Caleb kisses down my neck to the V of my blouse, half lifting me before rolling me over onto the drop cloth, holding me down as he kisses his way to my nipples, which are poking and aching against the cups of my thin bra. "You—" Caleb murmurs before sucking and nibbling at my nipples through my clothes, causing my already pebbled tips to become painfully hard, begging for more. I reach down and hurriedly unbutton my blouse, tempted to rip the whole damn thing off except that I don't have another shirt in my car. Caleb raises his head enough to let me sit up to shrug it off before he unhooks my bra, and I arch, trying to press my now naked upper body against him. Caleb sits back more, a look of wonder on his face.

"Fuck, Cassie, you're gorgeous."

I grin, grabbing his shirt and pulling it off him before replying. "More pew pew, less Q Q," I growl, grabbing his head and pulling him back to my breasts, where he licks and massages them, back and forth. His hand starts to trace down my stomach, toward the button of my work slacks, expertly unhooking it and sliding the zipper down. Slipping a hand inside, he cups my hot, quivering pussy, causing both of us to groan in pleasure. "Holy shit, yes!"

"Mmm, feels perfect," Caleb growls against my breast as his thumb starts rubbing my clit in little circles through my panties, driving me wild. I'm already soaked, and I know he can feel my wetness. He doesn't stop, and he kisses his way back up to my lips, claiming me with a searing, possessive kiss that leaves me breathless.

"More . . . I need more," I moan incoherently, running my fingers through his hair and looking up into his piercing eyes. God, if I'd known how good he was at this, I'd have tried this months ago. "Please, more than your hand."

Caleb nods, pulling back slightly, and helps me shimmy my slacks and panties down my legs, leaving me naked and him in his jeans. Somehow, the discrepancy makes me feel more on edge, more naughty. Caleb lifts my legs, settling between them and sitting back on his heels. His eyes focus on my pussy spread before him as his work-callused hands somehow still tenderly massage my inner thighs. His eyes find mine, desire flaring in them. "Tell me. Cassie, I need you to tell me to lick you. Because I need to taste you. I want your smell in my nose and your taste on my tongue."

I've never felt such impact behind a lover's words. The slight strain in Caleb's voice as his eyes travel up my body to find mine sends quivers through me. I reach down, grabbing his wrists and lowering my voice. "Yes. I want that. Lick me. Make me come all over your face." Before I can even finish, he bends forward and cups my ass, lifting my hips toward his mouth, meeting in the middle with an explosion of sensation from the first touch of his tongue.

I should have known from how good he kissed and how he made my breasts ache, but I'm not prepared for the electricity that jolts my body as he licks up my entire slit with the flat of his tongue, pausing at the top to give my clit a concentrated lick back and forth. After marking it with his tongue, he gets to work, the hungry snuffling sounds coming from his mouth giving testament to how passionately he's licking me.

His tongue never stops, driving me crazy as he traces patterns across my clit, sucks my lips into his mouth, and drives his tongue into me, tongue fucking me as I'm slowly driven wild, getting louder and writhing under his ministrations. He focuses on my button, sucking on it while he slides first one and then two fingers into my dripping wet pussy, stretching me as he pumps them in and out.

Warning tingles rush from my pussy through my entire body, and I throw my head back. Caleb tries to slow me down, but I'm too far gone, weaving my hands through his hair to grab him, grinding my pussy against his face, desperate. "Please, Caleb, I'm so close. I need . . ."

Caleb growls and lightly bites my clit at the same time he curls his fingers into my g-spot. Fireworks explode in my vision, and I'm sent hurtling off the edge into an orgasm, lights sparkling behind my closed lids. All I can do is hold on, moaning "fuckfuckfuck," over and over as the world seems to twist, reality disappearing only to reappear after what feels like an eternity later. Opening my eyes, I see Caleb wiping my juices from his stubble, grinning. "Good?"

Caleb's laugh is sexy, the fire in his eyes even sexier. "That was the hottest fucking thing ever. Now it's your turn."

Caleb scoots back, and I sit up, pushing him lightly onto his back and marveling for another moment at the ripped muscles of his upper body, the lean trace of his narrow waist, and the tight muscles underneath. Everything is hard, and I marvel at the bulge in his jeans, biting my lip.

I stretch out next to him, tracing the muscles of his chest and stomach. Little goosebumps start to dot his skin as I get close to his nipples, making me hum in appreciation. "Mmm, someone is sensitive."

"Woman, it's been a bit too long for me as it is. I'm likely to come right as I get inside you. You might want to hold off on the teasing a bit," Caleb admits, and for some reason, his honesty makes this mean more to me. I hear the zipper on his jeans, and I realize his pants are undone. I sit up, grabbing the waist and carefully pulling them down. Caleb helps, pushing his hips up so I can get them and his boxers off. Before I can toss them aside, he sits up, reaching into the back pocket to pull out his wallet, and takes out a condom. "Safety first."

Looking at him, I have an unobstructed view of him for a moment. His cock stands proudly, nearly reaching his belly button. He's handsome, but with the smile on his face, the ripped muscles, and the huge dick that's staring out at me, I'm in awe of him for the first time ever. "Holy shit, Caleb. How did I not know . . . you're fucking packing."

Caleb chuckles, opening the condom and rolling it down his shaft, relaxing slightly. "You always know just the right thing to say, Cass." Stretching out his long legs, I'm aware of what he wants as he opens his arms, and I dutifully climb into his lap, straddling him face to face.

Caleb looks at me seriously. "Are you sure about this, Cass? Just friends, no strings? Fuck buddies for now, friends always. Last chance—you sure?"

In answer, I lift up, impaling myself on his huge cock in one drop, making both of us moan in pleasure.

It's like nothing I've ever felt before.

CHAPTER 15

CALEB

*C*assie takes my whole cock to the hilt in one swoop, and I'm a goner. I try to let her ride me, control myself as she bounces on me, her pussy squeezing me and thrilling my cock from tip all the way to the base. She hugs her arms around my shoulders, bringing her tits to my attention, and I suck one nipple into my mouth, drawing on it deeply. The way her nipples feel against my tongue and between my lips is heaven itself. She moans, begging. "More . . . Caleb . . . please . . . fuck me."

She whimpers, and I can't hold back anymore. Wrapping my arms behind her, I hold her shoulders from behind, letting her lie back in my supporting arms. I roll both of us over, laying her out on the cloth, her hair spreading around her like an angel's halo, her eyes wide with the feeling of my cock grinding inside her. Getting to my knees, I fuck her deep and slow, pounding in with force, bottoming out and just holding her there, full of my cock, for a split second before doing it again and again. Cassie wraps her legs around my waist, holding me close, the pace increasing as I abandon myself to the sensations.

"I'm there, Caleb . . . so close," she moans, lifting a finger to my mouth. I take it in, licking the tip then watching raptly as she lowers her pink-tipped finger to her clit. She rubs slowly, in time with my thrusts, and the sight of my cock disappearing into her wet pussy, along with her rubbing herself, is just too much. I speed up, slamming harder and harder into her, our bodies shaking, until I come with the force of a freight train, holding her tight and immobile on my cock, grunting my pleasure as I see her finger move a little faster for a moment before she shudders in my arms too. I thrust a few more times, driving both of our pleasure on for as long as possible.

Time draws out, and as the balmy evening air cools our sweat-drenched skin, I hold her, thinking that in all my life, I've never felt anything like being with Cassie. Finally, we look at each other, shocked faces for a moment before she finally sets the tone, like she always has. "Okay, fuck buddies. I think this can work."

That right there is why we're friends. Inside, I'm swirling, trying to figure out if 'fuck buddies' is really what I want to be, but Cassie takes control and gives us some clarity. She always has throughout our friendship. Hopefully, we're not messing that up, but damn if I can't work with sex like this too.

CHAPTER 16

CASSIE

*T*he blistering heat envelops me as I step outside with a glass of cold water in my hand. Immediately, the humidity makes my thin cotton tank top cling to my body even before I'm halfway down the steps.

"I get it, I get it," I mutter to myself, glancing up to the heavens. "I've been such a bad girl that I have to spend the summer living next door to the gates of hell. Doesn't mean you have to throw in the mugginess too."

At least the weather's good for one thing, I think as I feel a droplet of sweat trickle down the back of my thigh. I can barely stand to wear anything at all, so I've spent most of the past few days in nothing but crop tops and Daisy Dukes. Sure, I might be looking just a tad bit skanky, but I think I can pull it off. And it's done wonders for my tan.

I hear the buzzing of the small gasoline motor, and I come around the corner of the house, knowing what I'll find. After a delay in getting some of the materials that we need, Caleb and I decided to tackle something else. A friend of his was willing to let us borrow his big riding lawnmower, so we're tackling the one-acre space behind the house, taking it from a jungle to a half-tamed space. We'll worry about making it a lawn later, but today's all about at least getting it so that I'm not worried about snakes or other creepy crawlies if I want to take a walk back here.

Caleb and I have been working together all morning to try and get the lawn done, alternating between driving the mower and using the other tools. We've been through six gallons of gas in the big mower, but the ten huge bags of cut grass stand as a monument to the amount of work we've accomplished. But now, he insists on running the weed whacker, saying my bare legs are in danger. The way he keeps looking at my legs and ass, I'd say he's the one in danger . . . and that's just the way I like it.

"Do you need some wa—" I yell, but the words freeze in my throat at the sight in front of me. Caleb's peeled off his shirt while I've been inside, leaving him in just a pair of jeans that hugs his lean hips like a glove, and I get a full view of the long muscles of his back and the swell of his arms and shoulders as he shuts off the motor. Just looking at the sweat glistening on his tanned skin makes my internal temperature ratchet up a few more degrees, and I'm tempted to drink half the glass of water myself. I'm burning up inside.

"Hey," he says, turning all the way toward me and shrugging off the gas trimmer. Watching his chest and arms flex with easy strength and the bead of sweat that trickles down his pecs before coursing its way over the deep ridges of his abs has me gasping for air.

I've always known that Caleb was a fine, sexy specimen of manhood. But the recent change in our relationship has me looking at him differently. I'm shocked at how turned on he makes me. These past few days, I've noticed him not as an opponent, not as a playmate, but as a man. And no matter how much I want to deny it, I want him with every fiber of my being.

Why couldn't I see this before? It makes sense. From the moment I saw him, I wanted to beat him, to show him that I was worthy of his notice. Every mean trick I played on him, every time I've tried to show him up since we've started working together, it's always been to get his attention. Sometimes, I've been subtle, like with a slight joke or making sure I wore my thinnest bra today underneath my thinnest tank top. Other times, it's been as in your face as a bucket of water poured over his head. Yeah, I did that too.

And now, I can't deny it. I can't get enough of him.

The corner of Caleb's lips curl up into a cocky grin as he watches me, and I realize I'm staring at him, the glass of ice water frozen in my hand. "You okay?"

I tear my eyes away from his sweaty abs. "Yeah, a bead of sweat just fell in my eye." I lie my ass off, trying to maintain at least a little bit of control of myself. I'm not quite that desperate that I want to fall on my back in the freshly mown grass and spread my legs, begging him to plow me. At least, not yet. I wipe at my eyes with the back of my hand, holding out the glass of cold water. "Here. You look like you need it."

Caleb reaches out and takes the glass from my hand, my eyes fixed on his Adam's apple as he downs half the glass, his throat making me even more breathless before he stops and gives me a curious look. "You sure about that?"

He steps closer, and he's so close I can feel the heat emanating from him, heat that has nothing to do with the blistering sun. I swear my internal thermometer is rising through the roof. Standing next to him, the only image I have in my head is of my entire head exploding like a cartoon thermometer, but I can't tear my eyes away from him.

"I'm sure," I finally reply, my voice husky. "How much more do you have to do?"

"Not much," Caleb admits, not looking anywhere but at me. "There's a few bushes that need trimmed, but that won't take long at all."

If you want to see a nicely trimmed bush, I've got one for you, I think, but instead, I nod. "Okay."

The sounds of the summer fade away as I watch him finish off his drink, a trickle of water running from the side of his mouth and down to his chest, making me want to lick the clear droplet off his skin. He licks his lips, and all I can imagine is feeling his hands, his lips, his tongue licking me that way, and I moan lightly, my thighs trembling with desire.

Caleb finishes the last bit from the glass before crunching

one of the ice cubes that I'd put inside, smiling. "Delicious. Just what I needed."

Please, please, PLEASE run that ice cube over my nipples, I want to beg him, my heart pounding in my chest like a sexual drum. "Yeah. I was just going back inside. I was going to get that list of stuff for the bathr—"

Trying to keep my eyes in a safe place, I fail utterly. Every glance at Caleb makes me want him more, and I stammer, unable to find a single square inch of his body that doesn't leave my heart fluttering, my stomach twisting, and my pussy aching. Finally, in a desperate bid for keeping control, I turn to leave, but I freeze when I feel a powerful hand grab my wrist.

"What are you doing?" I gasp as Caleb pulls me back around, my body pressing against his. I can feel his heart pounding against my chest, and between his legs is a throbbing, thick heat that leaves my knees weak.

Caleb grins at me, his eyes twinkling in a way that I've never seen before. "You didn't call me names like you normally do."

"Oh," I whimper weakly. "I just forgot. This heat has me burning up."

Caleb lowers his lips until I can feel his breath on my ear, and I whimper again, my nipples hardening inside my top. "I think you're burning up all right. And I know just what to do about it."

"Oh, is that so?" I ask as my hands clutch at the full, hard muscles on his chest.

"It is," he purrs, pressing himself into me. I can feel the rapidly hardening growth of his cock, and my legs seem to spread on their own to let him have access to me. I want him so damn badly I can taste him already.

He pulls me tighter, and I moan, unable to form words. He's got me right where he wants me. Caleb whispers in my ear, "You have a problem, and I have the tool for the job."

He grabs another one of the ice cubes from his glass, gently dropping the glass to the grass. I bite my lip as he brings the ice cube to my jawline, tracing the line and then letting the drops run down my neck. He dips his head down to lick at the river of drops from the quickly melting ice, humming in satisfaction.

"Mmm, even more refreshing than I thought. Are you cooled off now?"

Knowing it'll drive him crazy, I smirk and shake my head. "Not even close. In fact, I might be even hotter now."

"We can't have that, now can we?" he says as he trails the little bit of remaining ice down toward my cleavage. I press my tits together, creating a little crevice for the water to puddle, and Caleb's eyes focus there. Moving his hands over mine, he cups my breasts together even higher, lowering his head to dip his tongue into the pool, lapping the water up and running his tongue along the upper crest of my breasts. My head falls back as I groan. The water gone now, he moves to slip the neckline of my tank down, giving him more access. Kissing down, he slurps my nipple into his mouth, swirling his tongue over the peaked tip. He's driving me crazy, and I know my panties are already soaked.

I'm this close to letting him take me right here in the backyard, whoever can see be damned, when I hear my phone blare out. *"Work hard, play hard."*

"Shit," I gasp, pushing away from Caleb and going over to his truck to grab my bag off the tailgate. My phone's still singing its digital ass off, and I know from the ringtone that it's work. I pull it out and see that it's Martha. "Fuck!"

"Well, that was sort of what I had in mind," Caleb teases, grabbing my hips from behind and pulling me closer, but I pull away before I can be swept away in the sexual passion coursing through me.

I hold up a finger to signal for him to hold on a second, answering the call. "Hey, Martha, what's up?"

Caleb realizes it's work and is professional enough to not do anything too naughty. Good boy. "Hey, Cass," Martha says. "I hope you're not waiting on me."

Oh, shit, I forgot . . . Martha is supposed to come to the house today. It's a good damn thing she didn't pull up just now or she would've gotten a bit more show than she'd planned on. "Oh, um, no, Martha, not at all," I quickly reply while trying not to facepalm myself. I've done that before, and it's not a good thing to do while you have your smartphone to your face. "Actually, we're just finishing up the yardwork. Why?"

"Well, I guess we're both lucky then," Martha says with a relieved sigh. "I was getting my hair done, and you know how the salon can get on the weekends. Is there any way you could meet me at the office in an hour instead of my driving out there?"

"Yeah, no problem," I say, relieved. "I'll see you there."

We hang up, and I turn to Caleb, who looks disappointed. "Sorry."

"Work?" he asks, and I'm counting the minutes in my head even as I look down. An hour. That means we have about ten minutes to . . .

No, stop it, dammit, I tell myself.

"Yeah, work. I promised Martha I'd go over some documents with her. She's gotta send them off Monday morning or else."

Caleb sighs but nods. "I understand. Well, at least I know I can make you lose all track of time."

I laugh, shaking my head. "Probably because you're so boring you put me to sleep."

"Is that what you call it when you scream my name and pass out? Boring. I'll remember that."

I walk into Mindy's Place fifty minutes later, my skin finally having stopped sweating after running my A/C on full blast from the moment I left the house. I didn't even have time to stop at my apartment. Luckily, I've taken a tip from Caleb and have learned to keep a clean t-shirt in my car along with some wet wipes. All I had time for was a quick wipedown and to sweep my hair back into its messy bun again. I feel bad about leaving Caleb behind with a lot of work and a very hard cock, but it can't be helped.

"Hey, those legs are dangerous!" Mindy calls from the counter as a greeting. "Showing off like that, I'm gonna charge you for every dropped cup of coffee you cause!"

"Don't be jelly," I tease, "and gimme something tall, dark, and icy as hell!"

"One Arctic Midnight Coming up for my Sexy Star," Mindy says. "How big?"

"Big enough to quell the flames inside me," I reply. I see someone glance over, and realize that Emily, Mindy's babysitter, is here. "Oh, hi, Emily."

Emily and I have been pleasant and polite to each other, but she's been pretty shy most of the times we've talked. It's no different this time either. "Hi, Cassie. Uh . . . how're you doing?"

"It's hot, I need cold caffeine, and I'd rather be riding a lawnmower tractor right now," I admit with a laugh, not saying what I really want to be riding. "What's got you here?"

"Oli took the kids out for a little bit of shopping and Daddy time before he and I have a date night," Mindy answers, grinning. "Since Em's agreed to watch them on a weekend, the least I could do would be to throw in some free lunch."

"Shopping?" I ask, and Mindy nods. "Don't tell me, Spocky's ears are poking through that hat I got him."

"Why do you always insist on calling my son Spock? His name is Zach." Mindy says, even as she grins. "It's not his fault that his ears are big for his age."

"Nope, one hundred percent his parents' fault," I agree. "Seriously, though, he's the most adorable little boy ever."

Emily gives us a double-take, then shakes her head. "I've heard you two are hard to understand."

"Just wait until you spend time with my sister," Mindy says. Before Emily can answer, the door to the cafe opens again and Martha comes in, thankfully also wearing jeans and a t-shirt, although her hair is freshly done. She's dressed casually, but she looks great. Mindy immediately whistles. "Whooo, someone's got a new man!"

"I do not!" I protest before I can even stop it, causing all three women to look at me in surprise. *Shit. Mindy was talking to Martha, not me!* "I mean, um . . ."

"Uh-uh," Mindy says, rounding on me and grinning. "Too late now. Spill it."

"That explains the glow," Martha adds. "And you do look a little perkier than usual."

"You have a boyfriend?" Emily asks in a rush before muttering under her breath, "Lucky."

"I don't have a boyfriend," I mumble, knowing I'm trapped. "I just—I've been . . . well—"

"Oh, for heaven's sake, girl!" Martha says, chuckling,

"we're all women here. Just spill it before my perm goes all to hell!"

"Okay, okay. I've been spending a lot of time with Caleb recently, as you guys know."

"Duh," Mindy says. "Wait . . . really?"

"What?" Emily, who spends most of her days with pre-preschool children, asks cluelessly.

"Well, boyfriend or not, someone's getting some, and it's about damn time." Mindy says, smirking. "Don't lie. Guess he's got some power in his tool bag?"

"Mindy!" Martha chastises, looking around, but it's an empty house at the moment. Figures. They have free reign to interrogate me. "How long have you two been together?"

"We're not *together*," I protest, perhaps a little too strongly. Emily chuckles, sipping at her drink while Mindy grabs mine and pours it into one of the classic soda fountain glasses she uses for her iced drinks.

"So if Miss Emily here went and asked him out on a date tonight, you'd have no problems?" Martha teases. When I growl, she chuckles. "Thought so."

"Hey, leave me out of this!" Emily protests.

Mindy waves her hands, trying to quiet everyone. "The important question is, are you going to leave us sitting here in suspense or are you going to give us details?"

"There are no details," I grumble, but I can't keep the smile from breaking across my face. "It's just casual between us, okay? We've got . . . you know, needs."

"Casual or not, anything good enough to make you smile like that is worth doing . . . again and again. And needs?" Mindy says, lifting an eyebrow. "Honey, chocolate is a need. Hot baths are a need. Hell, my frappes are a need. What you're talking about is a lot more than that."

"Well, you make some damn good frappes!" I counter.

"And I bet they'd be even more better if you were licking one of her frappes off Caleb's chest," Emily murmurs shyly. When we stare at her, she blushes deeply before replying. "What? Saw it on TV once. This guy took this super-thick Italian-style chocolate drink and poured it over his girl's belly and then down—"

"Emily is a secret little freak. I'm liking you more by the second!" I interrupt, but damn, her description reminds me of Caleb and what he was doing with that ice cube just before we were interrupted.

"Ladies, I hate to break this up, but if you don't mind, can Cassie and I head upstairs? We need to get a few things done," Martha says. I give her a grateful look as Mindy sticks out her tongue and follow Martha up to the office.

"Thank you. That was getting to be a bit more than I expected," I admit as Martha turns on the lights and powers up the computers. "I'll have those files for you in just a minute."

"That's just fine," Martha says, sipping her drink. "If you don't mind my saying, watch yourself, Cassie. You might be a little young for me to fully understand sometimes, but I like you, and I like Caleb too. Just make sure you both know exactly what you're getting into."

"I know," I reply, touched. "And we do." Martha's really taken a sort of half mentor-half aunt-like role for me, and I appreciate it. "So is that for anything special?" I say, nodding at her perm.

"The meeting with the investors from New York is next week," Martha admits with a chuckle. "Although if it doesn't work, I'll let you sing and dance for them. I'm sure they'd appreciate *Cass Gon' Give It To Ya*."

I roll my eyes, laughing. "They'd probably call security on me." I get the files quickly, sending Martha electronic copies as well as printing out the stuff she really needs. I sign a couple of places and point out the details she needs to make sure are covered in her investor meeting. Tapping the papers on the desk to get them lined up, I hand them to her. "Here you are. Anything else?"

"Just keep your phone on you in case I have questions later," Martha says. "Enjoy the rest of your weekend."

Downstairs, I see Emily still waiting for Oliver, and I give her a wave as I head out. I'm surprised when she follows me out. "Hey, Cassie? Sorry if you weren't ready to talk about things with Caleb back there."

"No sweat," I reply with a smirk. "I'm a big girl and it's my fault. I think I secretly wanted to tell someone."

"Yeah, well, I've only talked to Caleb a few times. But he seems like a great guy. You're already friends, and it sounds like you're, uh, compatible, so dating isn't too crazy, right? If you guys did decide to be more, I'm sure he'd make a great boyfriend."

Boyfriend. Sounds good, but not part of our agreement.

Before I can reply, a familiar-looking Lexus pulls in, and Oli gives a beep. "That's Oliver."

"Give the kids a big hug from me," I tell her, cranking my engine. I've got a lot of thinking to do, but also, I'm exhausted. I need to get home and chill for a while. As I drive, I have to laugh. Caleb and me, dating?

Don't be ridiculous.

CHAPTER 17

CALEB

*A*s the days pass, Cassie and I fall into a routine. Every day that I'm not working for another customer or only have a half-day, I'm over at 614 Douglas, working on the house. Cassie's there every Friday through Sunday, and she also pops in on the weekdays when she can. She earns my respect with her ability to get her hands dirty, and dirty is exactly what we do. It seems like every other night turns into our fucking like bunnies everywhere in the house, breaking in every room with our erotic sexcapades.

When the tile for the kitchen came in, we celebrated by piling the boxes up and my fucking her upright, her elbows planted on the pile to keep her balance while the whole house was filled with the sounds of our wild passion. When we got done sanding down the walnut floors, before we even bought the wood stain, we stained it with our sweat. It's like the more progress we make, the more we're ripping each other's clothes off.

Finally, after a month, I take a look around the house. I came in tonight because it's a Thursday, and my work for Oliver was easy, so I wanted to take care of some of the basics on the woodwork for the kitchen out here. Once the cabinets are up, I'll take care of the counters before we do the tile. I give a little hum of satisfaction. "You're looking good, old girl," I say, patting one of the doorposts. "See you tomorrow."

I shut off the lights and climb into my truck, feeling like everything is coming together nicely. Between Cassie's house and my other various jobs, I'm totally swamped with work, but she and I seem to find plenty of time to bring each other to new orgasmic heights. Even after going at it all of these times, each one is just as amazing as the first. Even better, we're still friends afterward, giving each other shit lightheartedly. When I got hit on by another customer, Cassie laughed her ass off right before swallowing my cock all the way to the base and making me fill her mouth with a full load of my cream.

The only thing not going so great is my diet. A few too many nights of pizza and Chinese take-out have me feeling a little like a slug. I'm not getting chubby—I'm working too hard for that—but I just feel lethargic, especially in the mornings. I know what I need to do. I'm going to convince Cassie to do a little speed work at the high school track. Maybe some runs up and down the bleachers will do wonders. Hell, maybe I can get Cassie to fill one of my teenage fantasies and we can go for a quickie under the bleachers. I can picture her with her running shorts pulled down around her thighs, just enough to let me in as I pound into her from behind.

Stopping that train of thought as my jeans get a little too tight, I switch gears to make a mental note of things I need to pick up at Home Depot in the morning. We've got another busy weekend ahead of us. Going inside, I lock the door behind me, flopping onto the couch and crossing my feet, dirty boots and all on the coffee table. I'll get some dinner right after I relax for a minute.

It's not until I've watched the second episode of some crappy sitcom, eating the last of my pork chop and apple-spinach salad, that I realize it. I'm alone, and for the first time in a long time, it feels . . . lonely.

I wonder what Cassie is up to tonight, and for a split second, I consider texting her. That's what fuck buddies are for, right? Booty calls. Hell, even if not for sex, that's what friends are for. To call to hang out when you're lonely.

I pull out my phone, but my thumbs freeze before I can type out anything. A nagging question rises up in my mind, and I stop. What am I calling her for? For sex? To hang out? For something else? What is Cassie to me now?

When I don't know the answer for a beat too long, I decide that maybe a night off is exactly what we need. I don't want to blur the lines, especially with a friend. Besides, I'll see her in the morning at Mindy's. Maybe we can reschedule our run for Saturday too. That way, we can start the weekend off on the right step . . . and if I'm lucky, under those bleachers.

CHAPTER 18

CASSIE

*J*ogging up to the park, I'm excited to see Caleb. It's been a couple of days since I checked in on the house or got off on his cock, and the way he invited me to run today instead of our normal Sunday, I'm excited. Although he did sound a little disappointed when I said I don't like the high school track and prefer the park. Dunno why, but it doesn't matter now.

I've been surprised at how well both sides of our relationship have been going. The house is still in that hollow stage, but Caleb gets what I'm trying to do and is working with me to create the design I see inside my head. All the demo and some of the repairs are done, and the house is starting to look like an actual house again, except for the bathrooms, which we still need to totally do.

And as for the sex . . . mind-blowing. If I'm honest, it's the best I've ever had by far. It's been the reason that I've been worried, too. Because sex with Caleb is absolutely addictive. I keep finding myself thinking about him, looking forward to the next time we get together, to the point I've even stopped by the house on weekdays if I know he's going to be there just to try and have an excuse to see him. I don't know, maybe that's gotten me clingy, and I was starting to feel a tad worried. But his invitation to run reassures me. Just like old times.

I don't want to think about the expiration date of our arrangement. I know it'll be hard to ever top it, so I'm gonna enjoy the fuck out of it while I can. Caleb is a total commitment-phobe guy, but surely, he won't stay that way forever. I get it, some girl in his past burned him badly. He mentioned her name in passing once, but I forget it now. But he's too damn decent and sweet to be a casual guy forever. He's going to get swept up in some woman's web, and that'll be the end of our fuck-buddy setup. I just hope that when that happens, we stay friends. I'd really hate to lose our friendship over some jealous bitch who can't handle his having a friend with a vagina. Admittedly, the fact that he knows that vagina intimately might be a bit of a complicating factor, but we'll cross that bridge when we get there.

As I jog to our meeting point in the park, I see Caleb from afar. He's stretching, lunging deeply, sticking his ass out behind him, and I wish for a second that I were behind him to give a little smack.

As I stare, I see a gorgeous, lithe blonde bounce up to him. Her ponytail and tits bounce in time to her little jog in place, and I instantly hate her. She's taller than me, with either the world's best sports bra or gravity-defying tits that somehow aren't flopping around even though she's showing at least half of those cantaloupes off.

I can't hear them, but see her lips move, saying something to Caleb, and his face lights up into a bright smile as he talks back. They're flirting. He's flirting. Oh, fuck this!

I start to speed up to claim my territory . . . *back off, Blondie Bitch*. I take about four steps before I stop with a thunk in my heart. Shit, I can't do that. That's not what we are. He's not mine to get all territorial over. We said that we'd be just buddies, working off the sexual needs without the relationship bullshit. But there's no denying to myself that I'm jealous as fuck.

As I struggle inside, I see her pull her phone out of her cleavage . . . *really, bitch, that is just unsanitary!* She types something, and Caleb looks down at his phone, holding it up to show he got her message. With a prissy little wave, she bounces off, and I want to swing her around by her ponytail so damn badly.

I squash the feeling down, jogging up to Caleb. He gives me the same smile, but a little side hug of greeting, which somehow hurts. Flirting with boobs in your face, but I get a side hug? Damn, that's some cold shit, Caleb.

He doesn't notice and steps back, giving me his normal casual smile. "What are you feeling today? Same path as usual?"

Usual? I'm going to need something a little more intense after seeing that. "Actually, maybe something a little different. I've got some pent-up energy I need to work out."

"Mmm, pent-up energy, huh? I know just the thing," Caleb says, making me feel even worse. He's just trying to have fun, and that's all I am, fun. He goes to grab my ponytail, my limp ass ponytail I messily gathered at the nape of my neck before heading out this morning. It feels flat compared to Blondie Bitch. I pull back, all of my swirling emotions turning into a snippy anger.

"Whatever, Old Man . . . just try to keep up." I sprint away down the path, and Blondie had better hope she's a fast runner. I might just put a foot up her ass the way I'm feeling. It's only seconds before I hear Caleb's footsteps fall in next to mine, but I keep my eyes forward.

We run in silence for a while, pacing each other easily. I have no plan other than to run my jealousy out before I talk to him. As we pass a playground, I gesture to turn off into the dirt path through the woods because I need another mile at least to get my game face on. As we dip behind the dense tree line, there's a sudden wash of quiet and peace as the forest surrounds us. Slowing down to account for the rougher terrain, our breathing evens out.

"So, what's with you this morning? Decide to train for a marathon you forgot to tell me about? I thought I was going to have to wave the white flag back there. You almost dropped me."

I shrug, not daring to look at him. "Take a break if you need to. I can meet you for brunch if you want. Or maybe you have other plans?"

I try to say it casually, but it sounds a lot bitchier than I intended. Caleb jogs a couple more steps then hops in front of me, forcing me to stop with his hands on my shoulders. "What's going on? What the hell did that mean?"

I refuse to meet his eyes, looking away into the woods, because if I look him in the eye right now, I'm not sure what he'll see. Anger? Hurt? Sadness? Whatever it is, it's not part of our agreement and not what I should be feeling. "Nothing. I'm fine."

Caleb grabs my chin and gently brings my eyes to his, and I find myself lost in his eyes instantly. I can't help it. He's so handsome, and the way he's looking at me right now, it's stirring me up inside. "If it's one thing I know, it's that when a woman says things are *'fine',* it means things most definitely are *not* fine. What's going on?"

I sigh and shake my head, forcing nonchalance into my voice. "It's really nothing, Caleb. Everything's okay. I just saw you talking to Blondie Bitch and thought maybe you'd want to have brunch with her. It's all right if you do. I've got stuff to do at home anyway."

Caleb gives me an appraising look, then laughs. "You're jealous. You're fucking jealous!"

I scowl, trying not to punch him in the gut to hide my embarrassment. "I'll admit I had a little flash of insecurity at the perkiness of her ponytail, but she's beautiful. Make sure you ask her what shampoo she uses for me when you talk to her again, 'kay?"

It's killing me to say it, but he's gonna move on eventually anyway. Maybe sooner is better than later, less painful at least. Caleb, though, is smiling at me like I'm saying something hilarious. "Cass—"

I cut him off, drowning in a storm of emotions that I have no idea where they're coming from. I just really want him to go away. I'm not used to feeling this, and I don't want to make things worse. But at the same time, the idea of his leaving just makes me more miserable. "Really. I need to do laundry anyway if I want underwear to wear to work Monday."

Caleb steps closer, crowding me with his body, making me step back off the trail and into the trees. I stumble slightly, slipping on the pine needles, and any second now, I know I'm going to be trapped against a tree. Caleb, though, just keeps looking at me with those eyes of his, his freshly trimmed jawline tight and so kissable. "Cass . . . stop talking. I don't want *Blondie Bitch,* as you called her. Where do you come up with these names?"

I think he's asking rhetorically, not really wanting an answer, so for a change, I do as he asks and shut up. Besides, I'm trying not to fall on my ass.

Caleb continues. "Her name's Brittany, and she just started talking to me and was nice. I didn't see the need to stomp on her feelings, so I gave her my snapchat and she sent me a friend request. I'll just decline it later and no harm, no foul."

"You mean you're not going to see her? Why? I mean, did you see her fucking ponytail? I was serious about that. I really do need to know what shampoo she uses." I'm trying desperately to backpedal, joke, and lighten this up before my jealousy goes and fucks up a good thing. I can't believe I got jealous. What the hell is wrong with me?

"You know my favorite kind of ponytail?" Caleb says, his voice dropping to a sexy growl that freezes me in my tracks. He steps closer, reaching behind me and wrapping my decidedly less glamorous tangle around his fist. He looks me dead in the eye, compelling me to meet his eyes. He pulls on my hair, forcing my chin to lift. Right before he kisses my neck, I hear him growl, "Your ponytail . . . it's like a fucking handle just for me to pull you right where I want you."

He uses my hair to gently guide my head back and forth, kissing and licking the saltiness from my neck and sending my heart hammering, heat flooding my body. I can't help it. I moan as he licks up the side of my neck before tracing my ear. His lips right on my ear, he whispers, "Turn around, hands on the tree."

Instantly, I obey him. Who the fuck am I and who does he think he is? I don't know, but my pussy knows exactly who is because I feel the gush of my juices at his command. Still holding my hair, he kisses my shoulders, his other hand tracing my curves, tickling along the side of my left breast. Lightly, he pulls my hair, forcing an arch in my back, my ass pressing into his groin, and I feel his cock, hard and ready. I'm really making him that hard looking the way I am when he saw Blondie fewer than twenty minutes ago? Talk about a boost to your ego. I groan, wanting to feel more, wanting him to fill me, and he grinds against me, the layers of clothing feeling like too much, keeping us apart.

Caleb growls into my ear, amused. "Did I hear you right? Are you saying that you're going commando in these little shorts that damn near show a peek of your delicious ass with every step you take?"

Embarrassingly, I whimper and nod. I know, I'm terrible with laundry. Twelve work outfits, eight sets of undies. The math doesn't work out. Caleb groans sexily and grinds his cock harder against my ass, his voice raspy. "You're killing me, Cass. I didn't know your sweet little pussy was just a slip of fabric away. Naughty girl."

Before I can even process what his calling me naughty does to my body, he smacks my ass hard with his hand. I cry out, but it's not in pain. Just a delicious sting that makes my pussy clench. I arch again, silently begging him to do it again.

"Mmm, I think you like that, don't you? Are you wet for me? Your sweet little pussy is dripping for me, isn't it? Right out here where anyone could see? Show me, baby."

I let go of the tree with one hand, moving to pull my shorts down. The air is cool on my ass, and goosebumps break out on my skin, immediately flaring to immense heat. I catch a glimpse of Caleb's eyes as he takes me in. He's primal, sexual, dominating, and intense. I couldn't tell him no right now even if I wanted, which I don't. I'm absolutely ready for whatever he's got in mind. When I get to mid-thigh, he stops me. "That's enough. Spread a little for me, but don't stretch out your shorts or you'll be going home naked."

The shorts hold me virtually locked tight, barely able to

make room for Caleb's hand as he cups my pussy. "Mmm, I knew it, you *are* soaked. You want me to make you come right here, don't you? In the woods where someone could come by any second and see how bad you are?"

"Yes," I barely whimper as he moves behind me, grinding against my ass as his fingers find entrance to my hot pussy. He pushes a single finger in and out, and I moan a little more loudly than I should out here. It's not his cock, but it's Caleb, and he feels so damn good that my arms are already trembling.

"Not too loudly," Caleb rasps hotly in my ear. He wiggles his finger, stretching me a little before adding a second, and starts pumping them in and out, making my toes curl inside my shoes. "I'm gonna finger-fuck you and you're gonna come all over my hand. But you've got to be quiet. Can you do that for me, Cass?"

All I can do is nod. I'm helpless to form any words. I feel him smile against my hair as he continues to fuck me with his thick fingers, speeding up and slowing down at his whim, leaving me breathless each time. As he curls them forward to brush against my g-spot, I have to bite my lip to muffle my cries. He moves his slippery fingers up toward my clit, circling all around it but not quite where I need him. I move my hips, chasing his finger, trying to guide him where I want him. Suddenly, his hand delivers another spank to my bare cheek, and I know that one will leave a handprint.

"You're not in charge here. I'll rub your clit when I'm ready, you hear me? Be still and enjoy the ride. Or I'll stop." I freeze, looking over my shoulder at him. He's still my Caleb, but there's something more there. He looks fierce, focused, his eyes burning with desire but also with a little smirk, daring me to challenge him.

With a grin of my own, I nod, trying to keep the cheekiness out of my voice and failing. There's no fucking way I want him to stop now. "Yes, sir." Caleb laughs lightly but returns his fingers to my pussy, now rubbing circles over my clit like I wanted all along. He might have gotten his way, but I definitely think I'm the winner in this battle, because holy fuck, are his fingers magic. "Mmm . . . sir."

I start to clench tighter, getting closer and closer. He covers my back with his body, closing in tightly, and whispers into my ear. "My naughty girl is about to come all over me. Right here in the woods, with her pants down, hair fisted in my hand. This is better than my first idea."

"Idea?" I moan, barely able to hold back. But I can tell Caleb wants to tell me . . . and I want to hear it too.

"Fucking you under the bleachers over at the high school stadium," he rasps, his fingers pumping faster. "Always been a fantasy of mine. But this . . . this is just as good. Sexy as fuck, baby. Give it to me. Remember our deal—keep it down, but come for me."

It's all I need. His calling me naughty, that fantasy, and his commanding me to come send me flying over the edge. I come harder than I've ever thought possible without him inside me. I clamp my jaw closed tight, holding in the screams, but the moans are still loud enough to be heard if there's anyone around. He flicks my clit through my orgasm until I collapse, begging for mercy. "Please . . . too sensitive!" I mewl, my knees unhinging. The only things holding me up are my hands and Caleb's hand in my ponytail. "Please, Caleb!"

I turn around and watch as he brings his fingers to his mouth, sucking my juices off and moaning at the taste. When he takes out the last finger, I catch his mouth in a kiss. His lips are tangy, and I melt into his hot, hard body. After a moment, he pulls back with a growl.

"Now we need some fucking pancakes," he says, starting to pull my shorts up for me. He gets to the bottom of my asscheek and stops as I reach down, cupping his cock through his shorts and massaging the thick, throbbing heat I find there.

"What? What about you?"

His hands shaking, Caleb takes my wrist in his hand and pins my hands behind my back. "I don't have a condom on me. It's in my wallet back in my truck, and the next time I come, it's going to be in that sweet pussy of yours. Not down your throat."

I smirk, biting my lip and looking up at him. "Why not both? Or maybe . . . you know, I've got more than one hole down there."

"Holy shit, you're killing me, Cass. Maybe we should get those fucking pancakes to go." With one last smack to my bare cheek, he helps me pull my shorts up and we run all the way to his truck. We head to the diner for two stacks of pancakes . . . to go.

CHAPTER 19

CALEB

*S*itting on the floor of Cassie's apartment, we drizzle syrup over our short stacks and settle down on the living room floor. There's a couch right here, but I don't think we've ever sat on it. The first time I came over, we sat on the floor, and it's just become a thing we do. I don't know why.

It's not important anyway, I think as I give Cassie a look. She's still in her running shorts, her leg cocked up, and I can't help it, my eyes keep being drawn to them, knowing she doesn't have anything on underneath. My cock is still asking when the fuck it's gonna get some action and why I didn't just try and fuck her as soon as I got my hands on a condom. But my stomach and brain are letting me keep calm . . . for now. They're saying let the anticipation build, let it draw out, and make it even better. "So, what's the deal with the house?"

Cassie finishes a giant mouthful of pancake and looks up. "What do you mean? It's a good project to flip. That's all."

I sniff the air, pretending, and she understands. I'm pretty good at detecting the smell of bullshit. "That is most definitely not all. I'm no expert, but even I know there's plenty of better prospects out there. Tell me about the house, about growing up there."

Cassie laughs a little nervously, shrugging in that way I know means she's not really comfortable talking about it. "Uh, I grew up there. I was little, and then I was bigger. And then we moved out right at the end of elementary school."

Nope, she's not getting away that easily. There's something about that house that has her by the short hairs, and I have to know why. For some reason, I think it's been the catalyst for the change in our relationship. "Damn, Cassie, you are tighter than a submarine, and I don't mean your pussy. Tell me *something*. Tell me your favorite memory there, at least."

Cassie goes quiet, and I give her time. She's not avoiding the question, just gathering herself, I think. She hums, then shakes her head a few times and finally settles on a memory.

"My eighth birthday. I begged and begged for a swing for the big tree out front and a vanilla cake with chocolate frosting. I woke up that morning, praying my begging worked. I woke up, and sure enough, Mama had made me a cake . . . for breakfast. It was awesome, not one of the cheap box cakes but something she'd upped the quality on, all moist and sweet and fluffy and . . . well, it was the best cake I've ever eaten. It even had sprinkles on top and a little candle for me to blow out. I unwrapped my presents, some new socks I needed and a little knock-off Barbie doll from the dollar store. She was pretty, and I knew Mama was happy to have gotten her for me, so I yelled thank you and ran around the table to give her a hug. She was squeezing me tightly and whispered in my ear to take the doll out to the front yard. When I opened the screen, I could see it. A tire hanging from a rope, right where I'd dreamed a dozen times that it would be. I really did squeal then and probably jumped a little bit because she told me to try it out. I ran out and started swinging. It was the best birthday ever. I've never felt more free than I did that summer, swinging in the tree, leaning back to stare at the sky. I felt like I was flying. I'd watch the sunset every night and then hustle inside right as the streetlights came on. It was the best summer ever," she finishes wistfully.

The emotion in her voice and the shine in her eyes touches me, and I can't help but smile back. She's so beautiful right now. "Vanilla cake with chocolate icing, huh? It's not red velvet, but I guess it's all right."

Cassie laughs and pushes at my shoulder. "Heathen. Red velvet? I'd rather have pistachio than red velvet."

I laugh, faking a retch before grinning. "The swing sounds awesome, though. Is that why you told Oliver that in your sales pitch? You want it to have a swing for another little girl?"

Cassie flinches a little, but it's a thought that's been running through my head for the past few days. A little girl, say one with hair just like Cassie's, with the same feisty attitude. I could see having a kid like that. Cassie finally nods too, sighing. "Mama always said it was a good family house, and I want it to have the family it always deserved."

My stomach clenches at the sorrow in her voice, and I quickly change the subject a little to bring her thoughts back to a lighter track. "Why was it the best summer ever? Did you not swing after that?"

Cassie sounds slightly distracted, probably lost in her memories, and her answer is both off-handed and surprisingly honest. "Oh, Ed bought the tire and the rope for Mama. So when he left, he took them with him."

"What?" I ask, half choking on the bite of sausage I'd started on. "Took the tire and rope with him? That's some pretty cold shit right there."

She shrugs. "Mama was a bit of a spitfire. I take after her. After Dad and her broke up, she decided she was gonna live life on her terms, no compromise. So she'd have a man for a while, then he'd be gone. A little later, she'd have another one. She never wanted to bend an inch, while at the same time, she always needed a man in her life. Trust me, it was frustrating, and I don't want to end up like that. There were some good ones, though, like Ed. He really was nice to me, despite his taking that tire when he left. And yeah, some were not so nice. It was never anything bad, just a bit of a revolving door of relationships that had me confused sometimes. Mama always said, 'Chin up. Fish are gonna swim away because swimming is their nature. That's why there's so many fish in the sea.' Took me a while to understand it."

"Wow . . . that's uh . . . deep and insightful, I guess. Did she ever fall in love?" I ask while secretly thinking Cassie's mom probably had the most self-defeating point of view in the entire world, my own included.

Cassie sighs, nodding sorrowfully. "With every one of them. She was heartbroken every time one of them left, too. But she was always there for me, taught me how to be independent. She wasn't perfect, but she showed me that love is worth having while you do, and to stay grateful for it every day."

"Where's she now? Do you talk to her? I've never heard you mention her before."

I nearly slap my forehead when Cassie stops, and I can see the glistening of tears in her eyes. She holds them back, but when she speaks again, her voice is a papery whisper. "No, she's gone now. After leaving here, we settled in the big city, and things were going okay. Mama had a new job. I seemed to have transitioned pretty well from a tomboy to a city girl, and then I moved out when I went to college. My senior year, she went on a road trip with her boyfriend, Steven. They were hit head-on in a freak accident and neither made it. It was rough because she was all I had in the world. Dad and I are on polite terms, but not very close. But I remembered what she told me and kept my chin up and the sun at my back, kept on keeping on. It's my motto."

I swallow, regretting the thoughts I had about Cassie's

mom just a few minutes ago. God, I'm an idiot. "Wow, Cass. That's rough. I'm so sorry. Your mom sounds like she was quite the woman."

Cassie nods, then smiles, bringing the seriousness of the conversation to a close. "Yep, so that's the house I grew up in. Me and Mama against the world. She always said it was the perfect little family house, and now I want to make sure it's ready for its next family. Swing and all."

As we finish our pancakes, talk returns to the renovations and what still needs to be done to get it ready for market. But in my mind, I keep thinking that I know a guy who owns a tire shop in town. I bet I could get a big pickup truck tire that would be perfect.

I'm surprised when Cassie leans over as I'm washing up in the kitchen. "You've still got a little syrup right there."

I start to wipe at my chin with my thumb, but her hand comes up, pulling mine away as she steps closer. "No, let me."

She leans forward, a mischievous spark in her eyes as she delicately licks the sweet stickiness off and purposely lets her tongue roll over my lips. The feeling of her tongue on my lips is electric, and I can't help reaching up to grab her ponytail again. It's so damn convenient and sexy.

"Mmm, keep that up and maybe I'll have another place for you to lick some syrup off me."

Cassie giggles as she moves her hands down to the waist-band of my shorts, pulling my quickly hardening cock out. "You don't need syrup for that. In fact, I think I might owe you one from earlier."

I put a finger under her chin, lifting her eyes to mine. "Cassie, you don't ever 'owe me one'. I feel damn lucky to get to lick your sweet little pussy and watch you come for me. This isn't tit-for-tat. We just take care of each other."

Cassie pumps my cock slowly, grinning. "I like the sound of that, but I admit I got kind of distracted at tits and tats . . . shirt off so I can see those tats."

I grin back. "Does that mean you're taking your shirt off so I can see those tits?"

"Duh!" Cassie laughs, and she sweeps her tank and sports bra over her head as I pull my t-shirt off. My gaze focuses on her breasts, reaching out to cup them in my hands and slipping a thumb across her pebbled nipples. Cassie moans but moves away, getting down on her knees and taking my now fully erect cock into her mouth just a little.

She licks and sucks the tip, swirling her tongue around the head before finally slowly lowering, taking my shaft deep into her mouth inch by inch. When her nose is nestled deep near the base, she lets out a satisfied hum, and I have to squeeze the base below her lips to keep from coming right then. As she bobs up and down, I lean back against the countertop, pushing her ponytail aside to watch her take me into her hot mouth over and over.

Seeing her looking up at me with those naughty, twinkling eyes, I can't hold back anymore. "Fuck, Cassie, that's a damn pretty sight. You're about to make me blow already." She hums again and I can't wait anymore. I need to be inside her. I pull my hips back slightly, and she looks up at me. "Cass, get up here. I need to be inside you."

"Well, we all have needs," Cassie teases, pushing her shorts down. "Now, what about the condom?"

"I paid for the pancakes, so I'm fully stocked and carrying," I joke, pulling out my wallet. "But if you keep looking so sexy and pantyless when we go running, I'm going to start keeping one in my sock."

"Lucky me," Cassie says, looking around. She pulls me over to her small kitchen table, lying back on it and spreading her legs. She's glowing, the lips of her pussy already spread. Cassie reaches down and rubs, shivering as she does. "You'd better hurry up and get that condom on, or else I'll just have to take care of what you started myself."

It's hard to focus on getting the condom wrapper open and down my shaft as I watch Cassie rub her pussy, slipping two fingers inside and moaning, teasing me as she slides them in and out. Finally, after what seems like an eternity but can't be more than twenty seconds, I step forward, pulling her closer to me, her butt helped by a placemat that gives almost no friction as I slide into her, Cassie's fingers pulling out just in time. We both gasp, and my eyes are pulled to hers. "You're right," I growl, filling her all the way in one long stroke. "Who needs syrup?"

"I can't last long," Cassie admits, her pussy squeezing me tightly. "I'm so worked up, sorry."

"Trust me, no more than I am," I reply, knowing that I'm

raging inside too. I start thrusting, pulling back and stroking hard in and out of her, our eyes never leaving each other as my cock throbs and pulses deep inside her. Cassie's fingers dig into my forearms as I speed up, my balls slapping against her ass we're fucking so hard.

The seconds seem to become minutes, and in those seconds I feel something, like a bridge is being built between us. Cassie's taking everything I have and loving it, while at the same time, she's giving everything she has to me. There's no misunderstanding, none of the frustration or miscommunication of earlier, just the look in her eyes as sweat breaks out on our bodies again, my cock pumping in and out of her, and the hammering pace of our sex.

I'm sure we don't last even two minutes, but it doesn't matter. When Cassie's fingernails dig in, I understand and reach down, rubbing her clit with my thumb. She gasps and her pussy squeezes my cock even tighter. "Caleb!"

"Me too," I gasp, my cock swelling before I come, Cassie's cries of her own orgasm pushing me even higher. Still, our eyes never leave each other's and I can almost feel what she's feeling, the heat and the explosion from deep inside different but just as intense and as needed as mine. When the moment passes, I stay inside her, reaching forward to stroke her hair. "Wow."

"And who says a quickie has to be bad?" Cassie chuckles after a moment. "That was . . . goddamn!"

I laugh, not wanting to pull out of her but knowing I need to dispose of the condom. "Come on, let's get washed up,"

I say regretfully. "Then you can get some laundry done while I'm at the house, and maybe, if you're really helpful, I'll even bring you some dessert tonight."

"Oh?" Cassie asks. "What's for dessert?"

"A thick, creamy banana."

Cassie laughs and smacks my naked ass. "Deal. And you might have a sweet muffin you can munch on too."

CHAPTER 20

CASSIE

*A*fter our confessional pancake brunch on Saturday morning, the crazy wooded adventure, and the mind-blowing sex, I was mentally and physically exhausted. Still a little embarrassed about my jealous fit and how emotional I felt after our couch session, I readily agreed when Caleb said he should probably head out. Taking a few hours to do all of my laundry helped, although I was disappointed when Caleb called later. One of his customers had an emergency issue, so he had to spend all Saturday evening and most of the day Sunday trying to repair a hole in the side of Mrs. Davis's house. Caleb even sent me a picture, although I have no idea just how the damn hole got there. But by the time he was done clearing out the damaged portions, repairing the wall supports, and then putting in the new drywall and exterior paneling, it was already near sundown on Sunday. He wanted to meet me at the house to keep on working afterward, but I knew he needed his rest and told him to hit the sack.

I was excited when he texted me last night, telling me that he made a good amount of progress on the projects Oliver has him doing, and he could be at 614 Douglas on Tuesday, so I'm heading over tonight. In his text, he begged me not to grab pizza, so instead, I've got some homemade chicken sandwiches, fruit, and a bottle of wine. I took the time to change clothes, so I'm back in jeans, but I also freshened my makeup and made sure my ponytail looks good. Actually, the idea of wearing a ponytail around Caleb has not left my mind. The way he pulled it and talked dirty to me has left me wanting more. Maybe that's why I brought the wine, and for damn sure, it's why I'm wearing some sexy, nearly see-through panties under my jeans.

Walking up to the door, I kick at it since my hands are too full to knock. Nothing, so I kick again, a little hard to do in my tennis shoes. Huffing in frustration, I set the food down on the porch to dig out my keys.

I know Caleb is here. His truck is in the drive. The handsome idiot probably has his music on loud again. As I get the door open, I move the food to the floor in the entryway, closing and locking the door behind me. Music . . . loud rock music from the back of the house. I figured.

Abandoning the food, I walk further into the house, following the music and the . . . singing? Stopping in the doorway, quiet as a mouse, I spy on Caleb. He's screwing drywall to the studs, and holy shit. Every time he presses the drill bit into the screw, his bicep flexes, his shirt sleeve up just far enough to let me fully appreciate the power in his arms. His corded forearms work and his biceps pulse, but the best part of the scene before me is not his muscles. The best part is the show he's putting on as he sings, nodding his head a little and even wiggling his hips as he stomps around. Damn, he's in the groove.

"Livin' it up as I'm goin' dowwwwwnnnn!" he sings, throwing his head back. He does a little slow turn and jerks when he sees me staring. He grabs at his chest, nearly hitting himself in the chin with his drill, and turns beet red. "Shit, Cassie. How long have you been standing there, gawking like a perv?"

"Oh, just long enough to enjoy the show. Who knew you could sing so . . . well? And such intellectual lyrics, too!"

Caleb's face turns an even deeper red, but he laughs. "Hey, I know I can't sing for shit, but it's a damn good song."

"I'm not hatin', but it's old man rock. That song hasn't been heard outside a strip club in decades."

"First, you say old man rock like it's a bad thing. Second . . . how would you know what music they play in a strip club? Got something to share with the class, Miss White?"

"Wouldn't you like to know?" I tease back, leaning against the door frame and stretching out all that my five foot one allows me to and sticking out my boobs until they're just nearly a respectable bump in front of me. "I've got some moves. Just because I never took my clothes off while I dance doesn't mean I can't shake it like a hundred-dollar stripper."

Laughing, I walk as sexily as I can toward him, pointing at his chest to stop him still. When I get close, I flip my hair around and sway my hips back and forth to the beat as *Aerosmith* gives way to *Pour Some Sugar On Me*, and I'm reminded that for Caleb, music decades are nothing more than suggestions. Caleb grabs my hand and twirls me around, starting a grinding partner dance. I'm surprised that he's actually a pretty good dancer, moving gracefully to the rhythm and turning us around but never losing contact with me as we grind. The feeling of his hips pressed against my ass is amazing, and my blood starts to pump harder in my veins as I feel a long, thick, and delicious bulge press against me.

"Is that what I think it is?" I tease, pressing back against him. Caleb responds by bringing a hand up and teasing the side of my left breast, breathing hard in my ear.

"You know exactly what it is," he says, rubbing a thumb against the soft flesh of my breast and sending more tingles through my body. "Now, were you a good girl or my naughty girl today?"

I gulp, loving the sound of his voice. *His naughty girl . . .* goddamn. "I guess you'll have to check out my panties to see," I reply, desperate to keep from tumbling out of control. "But first . . . dance!"

We keep going, teasing and toying with each other until the song crescendos to a finish with a throbbing hook and Caleb lip-syncs as he dips me in a final move.

He steps away while I'm left breathless and wanting to rip his damn t-shirt off—I'm so turned on—acting like he's accepting applause from an invisible audience. "Thank you, thank you. See you next year!" as he bows, then disappears through the doorway. I hear him yell back. "Elvis has left the building!"

I take a moment to inhale and let it out in a big laugh before I follow him back out to the living room for dinner. We settle down on two five-gallon paint buckets to eat our sandwiches and fruit from the brown paper bags I wrapped them in and drink our wine from plastic cups. It might be my favorite meal ever, to hell with the high-class restaurants. Give me this honest to goodness food, some good music, and most of all, a hot and sweaty man like Caleb. "That was hilarious. Who knew you could dance like that to '80s hair metal bands? I think I need to introduce you to some music from this decade though."

Caleb has a look of horror on his face and starts clutching at his chest in mock agony. "I'm doing just fine, woman. My musical taste happens to be amazing. You'll just have to learn to appreciate the genius of *Def Leppard*."

I wrinkle my nose, shaking my head. "We do like some of the same music, but yeah, I'm going with no thank you on that one. What's next, *Guns N' Roses?*"

"I was thinking *Twisted Sister*," Caleb says before breaking out in laughter. "No, just kidding on that one. Seriously, though, you know I'm not only a rocker. I guess I've always just associated do-it-yourself work like this with old rock. And when I'm smacking a hole in a wall or pulling up tile, that's heavy metal, *Drowning Pool* or *Slip-knot*. When I'm at the gym, it's hip-hop."

We finish dinner, talking about music from all decades and genres. We find some common ground in the great

Johnny Cash. Apparently, both our folks listened to The Man in Black, and it took root in our psyches, reminding us of happier times. That, and we both got the shit scared out of us watching the remake of *Dawn of the Dead* when we were younger and Johnny was the opening credit music there.

"Hey, I've got one last thing I'd like to finish today if you don't mind helping some? I need to tape and prep that back bedroom I just drywalled. If I get it done tonight, it'll be ready for paint before the weekend."

I drain the last of my wine, licking my lips in appreciation and nodding. It feels good to help out. "I've never done it, but I can help if you'll show me what to do." Five minutes later, I find myself with a roll of tape in hand, tearing off sections and holding them up as Caleb uses a putty knife to apply some kind of joint compound to the drywall seams around the room. Honestly, he probably could've done it faster without my help, but it's fun to do it together. I even get to sneak a couple of pieces on Caleb's back, forming the beginning of a smiley face. "We make a good team, you know that?"

Caleb rolls his shoulders, making the tape 'eyes' look like they're winking back and forth. "Yeah, well, you keep that up, and I'm going to be sending you to get a new roll of tape."

I laugh, sticking an 'eyebrow' on and stepping back. "A few bucks. I'm not worried."

"Hold the tape right here?" he asks, and I move under his arm, applying another piece while Caleb scrapes some putty into a spot. "That's the last one, I think. We do make a good team. It's been fun having you around more often than not. I usually work alone, only sometimes having day helpers for two-man jobs. I'll say, you're definitely the hottest helper I've ever had."

I wrap my arms around his waist, biting my lip and grinning. "Yeah, well, I hope I'm the only helper you've been driving your hammer into."

"For sure . . . Tony didn't swing that way," Caleb jokes, and I laugh. He pulls me closer, and we're about to kiss when he pulls back, a sheepish look on his face. "I probably should've told you this sooner, but you've got little flakes of dry joint compound all in your hair from leaning underneath me."

"Ew," I reply. "What's it look like?"

"Like you've got toothpaste in your hair," Caleb says, trying to pick some out. He gives up after a few seconds, shaking his head. "Too much. Sorry, I got you all dirty."

I reach down, cupping Caleb's cock and purring in a sultry tone. "It's all right. I like a nice hot shower at the end of the day. Your place or mine?"

CHAPTER 21

I drive as fast as I safely can to Cassie's apartment, ready to get cleaned up so we can get dirty all over again. Since the run in the woods and then the intense sex after the pancakes, I've been walking around in a constant state of arousal. Our little wooded adventure was such a powerful encounter, and then to be going at it again so quickly, I feel like I've overdosed on Cassie but I can't help but want more. I'm addicted, and I think she is too. The whole time we were on the table, I could see it in her eyes that she wanted me completely, that there was nothing we couldn't do in her mind. If it weren't for the repair job, we would have spent the whole weekend renovating and fucking, I'm sure of it. She was so hot and naughty, and the power of commanding her was heady, but an accident with a pressure cooker meant I had to spend sixteen hours repairing the damage and a Sunday night doing my best to rest my aching body.

It's been hard not jerking off, remembering how she came

all over my hand while struggling to stay quiet. The only thing that saved me was the comfort of knowing that we'd have time like this soon, and that tonight, I'm going to give her more than she's ever felt from me before.

She's such a good naughty girl. Even as she's closing the front door behind me, I'm already stripping in the foyer, partially because I don't want to get her place dirty from my work clothes and partially because I need us both naked . . . now. My cock is already raging hard, and Cassie's eyes go wide when she sees. "How can you even think with all the blood down there?"

"Right now, I'm only thinking of taking you to the shower and making you come all over my cock," I growl, smacking her ass. "Hurry up before I decide the clothes don't matter." She quickly follows my suggestion, dropping her clothes next to mine, and I scoop her up and throw her over my shoulder. She squeals in surprise, and I give her ass a little smack. "Let's get in, because I think I see some very dirty spots on you. I'll have to take care to get you extra clean."

Carrying Cassie through her apartment and to the bathroom, I set her down carefully, hopping in the shower behind her. I let her adjust the water to the temperature she likes before I turn her to face me, letting the shower run rivers through her hair as I smooth it, slicking it back from her forehead. I add shampoo, using my fingertips to massage circles on her scalp as she moans her approval. After a rinse, I repeat the massage with the conditioner. The whole time, my cock stands as a stiff prod between us, brushing occasionally against her stomach and sending a buzz through my body.

"Feels like you like washing me," Cassie moans teasingly, wiggling her hips back and forth and making my cock rub against her more. "After Saturday, too, I can for sure get used to this. You're so good with your hands."

"You should've realized by now that I'm more than just a handyman," I murmur. "Now turn around so I can wash your body."

She bites her lip and nods, whether in agreement or because she likes the idea of being washed, I don't know. She pushes her ass against the stiff root of my cock, making me gasp. Skipping the pouf, I pour a generous amount of body wash into my hands and start to lather them up. The smell of peaches with a little spice fills the shower, and I inhale deeply, enjoying the concentrated version of the scent that always covers Cassie's skin. I've come to associate it with her, a little bit sweet and a little bit fiery. Rubbing the suds all over her body, I pay special attention to her breasts, loving the way her nipples poke out of the suds and her sigh as I sweep my hands across and down her back, grabbing a handful of her ass on each cheek.

"Mmm, God, that feels so good," Cassie moans, pressing her hips back against my cock harder.

"Here, let me help rinse you off," I rasp as I move and direct her under the warm stream, rubbing the bubbles down and off her slick body. My cock is literally shaking with my heartbeat at this point, and I need a moment or else I'm going to come way too fucking soon.

"Now it's your turn," Cassie purrs, reaching down and wrapping a fist around my cock. "I'll make sure to wash you nice and slow."

I moan, pulling back. "I don't think I can wait, Cass. Fuck, I need to be inside you. Now."

"I won't argue with that," Cassie replies, letting go. I turn her chest to the wall, positioning her ass out as she arches her back. It's the sexiest thing I've ever fucking seen, the water splattering off her back to run down the curve of her ass before dripping between her legs, her hair pulled in front of her and the graceful curve of her neck outlined. "Time to give me what I want."

A flash of responsibility runs through me. "Shit, don't move. Condom!" I quickly gasp, hopping out, dripping water all over the floor as I start to run out to my jeans.

"Nightstand, top drawer. Hurry, Caleb!" Cassie calls before I'm even out of the bathroom. Not one to argue, I turn around, heading for her bedroom instead, and pull the drawer open to grab a condom. My hand is halfway in when I freeze at the sight before my eyes.

There's a few condoms, but that's not all. Toys. A whole drawer full of toys. Holy shit, Cassie has joked around before, but I swear she's got a miniature adult shop in here. Vibrators, dildos . . . something with two prongs, some other shit I don't even recognize. Naughty girl? Nope, I've found myself a genuine freak . . . and it's sexy as hell. My shock quickly turns to heat as I imagine her using these on herself, bringing herself to orgasm time after time. I grab one, pressing the button to turn it on, and then walk back to the shower, condom and vibrator in hand.

When I walk in, Cassie's washing herself, pulling on her nipples lightly and moaning, her eyes closed. She startles when she hears the buzzing, looking over her shoulder with a blush covering her cheeks. "Caleb, sorry . . . I didn't think about what else was in the drawer. Just meant for you to grab a condom."

"Why are you apologizing? It's hot as fuck to think of you using this on yourself," I say, climbing back into the shower. I run it over her shoulder and down between her breasts, and she moans thickly, her eyes locked on mine as I continue. "Rolling it over your nipples, teasing your clit with it, fucking yourself with it. My dirty girl . . . holy shit, I love it."

Cassie is still flushed, but it's less embarrassment and more desire. I offer the vibrator to her, and she takes it with a questioning look. "But—"

"Show me. Show me how you work your clit and tight little pussy with this fake dick before I give you the real thing."

With sudden understanding, Cassie grins, backing up against the wall of the shower and lifting a leg to show me her pussy. She does as told, starting with her already diamond-hard nipples, my eyes locked onto the point where the vibe touches her skin. She moves it down her body, using her left hand to spread her pussy wide, and grazes her clit with the strong vibrations. "Mmm, Caleb . . . you don't know how often I've had to come home and imagine your teasing me like this, my pussy so wet and tight, thinking of you, wanting to fuck you, to feel you throbbing inside me."

As her erotic voice continues, I can't stop my hands from moving to my cock, and I stroke up and down my shaft. I might not last long, but I'll be damned if I'm not gonna enjoy this show. Moving her hand, she teases the vibe tip around and around her clit, circling repeatedly before holding it still for a moment of intensity before starting the process over. She looks at me, waiting for me to tell her what to do next. "Fuck yourself with it. I want to see you take it deep inside. Get yourself ready for me."

"Yes sir," Cassie groans, moving the vibrator lower, just the tip disappearing into her pulsating pussy. "Caleb, I need you all the time. I want to be your naughty little slut."

"Do it, Cass. I can see your pussy trying to suck it in, wanting to be filled. Take it like my good girl."

She whimpers, and I correct myself, leaning to growl in her ear, "Take it like my fucking naughty girl. Do it, and I'll give it to you exactly how you want it."

She waits until I'm watching her pussy and then pushes the vibe in with one thrust, throwing her head back in pleasure. She pumps it slowly, pulling roughly at her nipples and moaning my name. I try to hold back, but my hand moves on its own, wrapping around my cock and starting to pump again. A couple of strokes on my shaft and I can't wait anymore. I jam the condom on as fast as I can, and the tight rim of the condom both makes my cock harder and pulls me back so I might last a few more seconds. I'm already on the edge watching her fuck herself.

"My turn. I'm gonna fill you up with my cock. But you put that vibe on your clit and rub yourself with it. Show me."

"Yes sir," Cassie whimpers, opening her eyes as I lift her up higher. It's dangerous, but I don't care as I pin her against the warm tile, positioning my cock and thrusting into her soaking pussy to the hilt, holding us both still for a moment to adjust. In the stillness, I can feel the buzz of the vibrator a bit through her pussy lips, and it damn near drives me insane. It's not like anything I've ever done before, and my mind wonders what other things Cassie and I could explore together and how much pleasure we can give each other. I start driving into her, my arms wrapped around her lower back to lift and drop her as I need to so that I can fuck her like I want, like she wants. I watch as she moves the vibe around her clit in tiny circles, but then she dips it down lower and it touches my shaft as I pull out and push in. I shudder and she grins devilishly. "Mmm, you like it too."

"That's new—do that again."

She does, circling her clit and rubbing my shaft with the vibe as we rush toward our orgasms. "We have a lot of exploring to do."

Cassie whimpers, nodding. "Fuck, Caleb, I'm so close. Please make me come."

"Hold it right on your clit. Get there, Cass. I can't stop. Come with me!" I barely get it out before we both yell, falling off the edge together, lost in the buzz of sensations coming from within. It's more intense than I imagined, and Cassie's digging her short fingernails into my shoulders as I hold her, impaled deep inside her. Leaning forward, I kiss her tenderly, letting our tongues slip and wrap around each other slowly before pulling out. I slip the condom off and throw it in the bathroom trash. Stepping back in, I shiver. "The hot water is totally gone, but I still need to wash my hair. And maybe you need another sudsing?"

Cassie chuckles and gives me a peck on the lips. "I think we'd never get out of here if you touch me with bubbles again. Not that I'm complaining, but I'm going to sleep like the dead after our day."

CHAPTER 22

*A*s I finish up in the bathroom, running a comb through my hair to make sure I don't end up with a rat's nest tomorrow, I realize that I don't hear Caleb. Curious, I quickly finish up before looking at my towel. Oh, to hell with it. It's not like he hasn't seen me do . . . well, he's seen me do almost everything, and I love it. The way he encouraged me, joining in . . . it's like I've found the perfect partner, and I'm starting to wonder if there's more to it than that.

Walking out to the living room, I see him doing up the buckle of his belt. He's already got his shirt, and I'm confused. "You're leaving?"

Caleb looks up, looking both slightly panicked and at the same time, guilty, like a kid who just got caught in the cookie jar and doesn't know how to react to it. Finally, he shrugs, dropping his hands to his sides. "I figured I'd better get going since you said you were tired."

His nonchalance seems forced, but it still makes my stomach twist, and I try to cover up my fear. *I'm not Mama, I'm not Mama . . .* "I thought you might stay. But yeah . . . okay."

Caleb hears something in my voice and stops, putting his hands on his hips and tilting his head as he questions me, "You really want me to stay?"

"If you want. It's late, and my place is closer to the house anyway." I try to make it sound casual, like it's not a big deal. But there's a swarm of butterflies in my stomach. I want him to stay, but I don't want him to stay because of me. I want him to *want* to stay. And now I even *sound* like Mama. *Shit. What happened to keeping it casual? Fuck buddies, no strings, just getting off when we need it? Remember that little statement? Slow your roll, Cassie.*

I sigh in my head, knowing that the little voice is just my fear talking, but I'm unable to shut it off. *What is wrong with me? I know better than to get tied up with a man who'll leave. Enjoy it while they're here.*

My heart does a little leap, though, as Caleb wordlessly pulls his shirt off and drops his jeans in answer, and follows me down the hall. When we get back to my bedroom, he pulls off his t-shirt, making my heart leap again. Pulling back the covers, we lie down, him on his back with my head on his chest. He mindlessly plays with my hair, twirling it around a finger and then letting it unfurl as his breath evens out. We're almost asleep when it slips out. I can't help myself.

"Tell me about her."

Caleb stiffens, his hand immediately freezing in my hair. "What? Tell you about whom?"

I shift a little so I can look him in the eyes, concerned that I might be opening the one can of worms that could tear us apart, not just as bedmates but as friends too. "The one who gave you the *Fuck You* t-shirt. I forget her name, but I know you said something. What happened?"

Caleb licks his lips, blinking as his mind pulls him back, and for over a minute, he stares up at the ceiling, reliving some small private hell before he replies softly, but with a harsh edge to his voice, "I don't really want to talk about that."

I look in his eyes for a moment longer, and part of me says I need to push the issue, but another side of me is afraid that if I do, he's going to get out of bed and walk out. Finally, I compromise. I cup his cheek, turning him to look at me as I sit up a bit more, and I lean over, kissing him gently on the lips.

"Okay, but you really shouldn't hold that stuff in. What-ever she did, let it out and move on. You're a great man. And I'm not talking as your fuck buddy or as your friend. I'm saying that as someone who cares about you. You deserve better than whatever she did. If you ever want an ear to listen, I'll be here. I promise."

I slide back down, turning over to tuck my pillow under my head. I can feel Caleb's heat behind me, but he's stiff, uncomfortable, and I start to regret even bringing it up. He is silent for so long, I think he's given up and fallen asleep. I'm just on the verge of sleep myself when I hear him speak quietly. "Her name was Wendy."

I don't dare say anything back, afraid if he knows I'm really listening, he'll stop. Still, Caleb turns on his side and lays a hand on my shoulder, and I turn over, looking at him silently in the dim light that filters through the window. I can see in his eyes that he's got a lot to get through. Still not saying a word, I shift and pull him to my chest, letting him rest his head on my breast. Caleb adjusts too, and I wonder if he's going to say more.

"We dated several years ago. I was in college. Even then, I was interested in more hands-on stuff, but I wanted to make sure I knew my business side too. I was more reserved back then, more interested in finding *the one*. We met my senior year, when I was looking at getting started with a construction company her dad owned. I wasn't really looking to get with her at first, but we hit it off well."

I say nothing, just trying to imagine a quiet, reserved Caleb. He's always been . . . I guess the best word is tranquil, but reserved? It's hard to imagine.

"I thought she was the one. I really did. We'd talked about getting married, having a family, and settling down, and God, I wanted that. I thought I wanted that with her. After I got my degree, I started full-time with her dad, and we started . . . well, we decided that we didn't need protection anymore. The day she told me she was pregnant was the happiest day of my life. I picked her up and twirled her around the room as I shouted with joy. As soon as I set her down, I dropped to one knee and asked her to marry me. I didn't have a ring or anything, but she said yes and I thought every dream I ever had was coming true. I got us a good apartment, and I worked myself to the bone with her dad to make sure I was bringing in enough money that we'd start family life off on the right foot. Wendy said she was happy, and I don't know, maybe she was at first."

He takes a deep breath, continuing. "A few months went by, and she was sick . . . so sick, throwing up morning, noon, and night. And I tried to help as much as I could, cleaning up the house so she could take a nap, making whatever she could stomach for dinner, but it was rough on her. We went in for a sonogram, supposedly to learn the sex of the baby. I remember being so damn excited. I had balloons in the trunk of the car, both *It's a Girl!* and *It's a Boy!* so I was ready either way. And I sat there in that fucking office, holding her hand as the doctor told us. The baby had stopped growing. There wasn't a heartbeat. I didn't need a fucking balloon. I was devastated, and I tried to hug her. She was stone-cold, no expression. I thought she was just too stunned, or she was being strong or something. She talked to the doctor about 'what next' and shit like that. I don't even know because all I could think about was that we'd lost our baby. The doctor excused himself to give us a few moments to grieve, and she let out a big sigh . . . of relief."

Wait, relief? Did I just hear him correctly? I still don't dare utter a word, but if I heard right . . . my heart starts breaking for Caleb, whom I can imagine putting himself through hell in order to take care of this woman. He'd have worked fourteen hours a day and come home to take care of her for another six if he had to. And she was . . . relieved.

"She wasn't overwhelmed like I was. She was just relieved. I tried to talk to her. I honestly don't remember what I said, but she got mad and loud. She started yelling at me, and I don't think she meant to say it, but she did. She yelled, 'It wasn't even your baby!' I'm not sure what hurt more, the fact that it wasn't mine or that she was already talking in the past tense. I drove her home, packed a bag, and never looked back. I called her dad, saying I was leaving, and he said he understood. He, at least, had integrity, and he even sent me two weeks' severance pay. I found out later that Wendy had been going behind my back the whole time I was busting my ass for her."

I swallow, tears forming in my eyes, but I don't let them fall. Instead, I stroke his hair, letting him know I'm here for him. Caleb clears his throat, his voice a little raspy as he purges himself of the last bit. "So I decided. The whole family with a picket fence thing is a lie. I thought I had my dream right in my hands and it imploded. Since then, no commitments. No getting tied down. I haven't told many people that story, and until I met you, I thought I could just keep cruising down the road of life, not worrying about it. Now . . . now I'm scared, because we're becoming something I never thought I'd be part of again. But yeah, been there, done that, got the *Fuck You* t-shirt."

Unsure of what to say, I say, "Caleb—" But before I can utter another word, he stops me.

"You asked. That's the story. I don't want to talk about it anymore or ever again."

I don't want to cause him any further pain, and I know how much it had to hurt to dredge all of that back up and pour his heart out to me. Quietly, I agree. "Okay."

With that, he takes a big inhale, settling down to sleep. There's nothing more to say, so I choke back my tears until I hear him start to snore lightly. Finally, I let them fall from my eyes, hoping the feeling of them striking his cheek and face doesn't wake him.

CHAPTER 23

I wake up like I always do, just before sunrise, to find myself in familiar yet unfamiliar surroundings. I have that foggy-headed moment of confusion . . .*What's going on? Where am I?* But as my brain clears enough, I realize I'm in bed with Cassie. Sigh. After the way she let me unburden myself last night, I couldn't just run out the door, even though I wanted to get away from the pity I'm sure she was hiding in her eyes. But if I'm honest, I slept better than I have in years. We snuggled for most of the night, but sometime this morning, we disentangled ourselves. I ease myself out of bed.

I've got a message on my phone, and after reading it, I decide to wake her up with the way I know best. Well, second-best, as the best would lead to sex, and I don't have the time for that right now.

"Good morning, sleepyhead. What's on your agenda for today?"

Cassie rolls over, sleepily brought up by the scent of coffee as I hold the cup out to her. She stretches like a cat, pushing her bare tits up at me for a moment, then grins and reaches for the cup. Tempting, oh, so tempting, watching her succulent body as the sheets pool around her waist. She's a woman a man could easily lose himself in.

"What time is it?" she asks before sipping the coffee suspiciously. Her eyes open wide at the first sip, and she blinks in surprise. "Wow . . . this is good!"

"I helped out at Mindy's Place for a week when she was out on maternity leave. She taught me a few secrets. And it's just after seven o'clock. Sadly, as delicious as you look right now, I've gotta get going. Ms. Steele sent me an urgent text message this morning, saying she's got an alarm going off and could I be the best handyman in the world and swing by and take a look? She probably just needs a battery, but I want to be sure. Knowing her, she probably took the battery out herself to have an excuse to check on me."

Cassie sips her coffee, looking at me in just my jeans, and smirks. "She probably just wants to check *you* out."

I laugh. "Nah, I think she wants to adopt me."

Cassie grins. "I need to head into the office too. I'll text you to see what's up later?'

"Deal. Make sure you get the paint colors to me as soon as you can. I've got some work to do for Oliver, but I figure I can get the texturing done within the next few days. I'll be ready to paint by this weekend." I tilt my head, putting on a fake affect and rolling my eyes. "It'll be so hard to cover up your hard work on the tape job, but it must be done, fair maiden. And with that, I bid you *adieu*."

Laughingly, I lean down to give her a kiss, and she squeals something about her breath, but I cover her lips with mine anyway for a goodbye kiss. Cassie smiles and gives me a little wave as I walk out of the bedroom, pausing at the door to turn back, giving myself a final glance of her as she sips at her coffee and looks at me with naughty, twinkling eyes. "Oh, hey, Cass . . . you need to do something about that coffee breath!"

I hear her laughter as I close the door behind me, and after grabbing my spare t-shirt out of the back of my truck, I drive back into town. As I drive, humming along to my music, I feel lighter, more energetic than I normally am at seven fifteen in the morning. Unfortunately, I have to skip going by Mindy's Place to get my morning sludge, but other than missing her insight on things, I'm not worried. I can stop by later, I guess, and grab something before taking care of Oli's stuff.

At Ms. Steele's, the beep of the alarm can be heard even outside, and she opens the door with the bright blue rubber of ear plugs visible in her ears. "Hi, Ms. Steele!"

She waves me inside, yelling at the top of her lungs. "Sorry I had to call you so early this morning, but I didn't know what else to do. I hope I wasn't interrupting anything. I just couldn't figure out what the hell was going on, and I can't even open the windows to let the sound out. The Tillersons across the street would call the cops if I did!"

"It's no big deal, I'm glad you called me," I reply, popping my own earbuds from my music player into my ears just to cut down the sound. I've got some heavy-duty ear protection in the truck, but I don't think it'll be necessary.

"Come on in and see what you can do about this racket because I'm about to take a shotgun to the damn thing. It's that newfangled one you installed a couple of months ago."

I step inside and see what she means. After Oliver had a gas leak at one of his properties, he had me purchase and install detectors at all of his rental units in town and one at his mother's house, too, just to be sure. I use a chair to climb up to the alarm, unscrewing the cover and removing the battery. The silence is beautiful until Ms. Steele lets out a loud whoop of celebration, extra-loud because she still can't tell how loud she is through the ear plugs. I pop a new battery in and the light shows green, problem solved. "Bring that chair on back into the kitchen. Breakfast is just about ready."

I smile, shaking my head, knowing she'd pull something like that. I love the woman and her breakfasts. They're the second-best in town. Only Mindy can lay claim to better cooking, and she's got a kitchen full of professionals to depend on. Sitting down in the chair, I drape a napkin over one leg and take a moment to look at the perfectly cooked cheese, bacon, and veggie omelet in front of me. "Ms. Steele, call me to fix something anytime if you're gonna feed me like this."

I tuck in, savoring the delicious flavors. More than just throwing a bunch of good stuff in the eggs, she knows how to balance all of them so that the saltiness of the bacon and cheese doesn't overpower the veggies, and the eggs are a fluffy cloud that supports it all. I'm not a chef, but I can appreciate good cooking.

She looks on in fond approval, then gets her own plate. "Well, I'm happy to have boys to cook for. Oli is so busy with work and Mindy and the kids, and with Tony gone off to Hawaii, I don't get to cook for appreciative folks much anymore."

There are a few moments of silence as I eat, and then she speaks up. "I talked to Tony last weekend. He said that he and Hannah are loving the island life, something about an addition, which I thought was his way of saying they're expecting, but apparently, he meant an actual addition to the resort. He was disappointed I wasn't more excited about some cottages, but really . . . compared to a grand-baby? Psh. I told him you and Cassie were working on a house project together."

I groan. I haven't told Tony about 614 Douglas for a reason. He's my best friend, but he can be a bit rough sometimes. "Oh, man, what'd he say to that?"

Ms. Steele smirks. She knows how we get along. "I think his exact words were that it's going to be explosive— either the house or y'all—and he'd lay fifty-fifty odds either way. Apparently, y'all have a tendency to needle each other?"

Fair enough. "Yeah, you could say that. Meeting under competitive circumstances probably didn't do either of us any favors, because we spent most of the first week we knew each other giving each other shit and teasing each other mercilessly. But we're good. We work together well and still tease each other more than is probably normal, but whatever. It's us."

Ms. Steele is looking at me with a shrewd look in her eyes. "Tell me about her. I don't know her other than in passing when I go into Oli's office. Mindy mentions her every now and then, but there's a difference between that and working together. Tell me more."

I pause for a moment, then start in, saying a little more than I intended to at first. "Well, she's a pain in the ass, always getting under my skin, but she makes me laugh a lot. We can just hang out and do nothing, but somehow, we always end up laughing our asses off, usually at something we said. She's just light, always smiling, and she makes people around her happy. And that's not easy. She had a bit of a rough upbringing—nothing major, but things that would've made a lesser person bitter or plain mean. She just lifts her chin and smiles at the world, daring it to go for another round."

Ms. Steele nods, sipping at her coffee. "She's a pretty girl. She always seems put-together when I go into the office. And in talking with Martha, she says that Cassie's always bringing a sense of humor to her work, too. Something about *Deadpool*, but I haven't seen the movie. Just the sort of girl that people like, though. I always wondered if she was seeing someone."

I swallow, not liking the thought of her seeing someone. "Yeah, she's gorgeous. Inside and out. But nah, she's not really seeing anyone. I don't think. Well, maybe kinda . . . but not really."

Ms. Steele laughs, half choking on her eggs. "I think that was the most non-answer answer I've ever heard. Caleb, are you and Cassie dating?"

I'm sure I'm turning a pretty violent shade of pink. I don't really know how to answer this one. "Uhm, no, not dating. Not exactly."

"Then what exactly . . . more than dating or less than dating?" Ms. Steele asks.

I shift uncomfortably, not sure how to explain the concept of fuck buddies to her. I mean, I know she's not totally innocent, but Ms. Steele's always struck me as the kind who sort of settled down and did things the old-fashioned way. She leaves me to squirm, then gives me a supportive smile.

"Caleb, if y'all are just having casual sex, it'd be fine. Despite what I can see you think of me, I had my own wild and crazy days. I'm old enough to be your mother, not your great-grandmother. I know what a hook-up is. But young people who are having casual sex don't talk about each other the way you just did about Cassie. I have a feeling you need to wake up and smell the coffee a little bit, young man."

I stammer, totally shocked by her words. They hit right at home. "Uhm, I don't know what to say. We're friends, and yeah, uh . . . we're a little extra-friendly sometimes, but yeah."

Ms. Steele waits for me to trail off, scratching at the back of my head before offering another question. "How often do you see each other? Do y'all do other things than be . . . extra-friendly?"

"Well, we see each other a lot right now because we're fixing up her house, so maybe four to five times a week. Oh, and we jog together and have pancakes on the weekends, usually Sundays, but recently, Saturday."

"Caleb, in my book, that's dating, probably neck-deep in a relationship, and you don't even know it. You get along, and you—ahem—*get along*. Sounds like a done deal to me. Congratulations." She finishes with a smirk as if she'd just solved all the world's problems. She waits for me to reply, then clears her throat. "Caleb, you know that Oliver's father and I are divorced, of course."

"Yes, Ms. Steele."

"Well, maybe Tony or Oliver has said what caused it, perhaps not. But regardless of what the boys think, the reality is that my marriage was over long before. We stopped doing those things together. We'd eat at different times, we'd do different things. We lived totally separate lives, apart from sharing a bedroom and occasionally being a little *extra-friendly*. So it probably was just a matter of time before things went the way they did. What I'm saying is that relationships can start mysteriously and end mysteriously. But to an outside observer, it's not that mysterious at all. Seeing the way you react when you talk about Cassie . . . you're looking good, boy. Scared, but good."

I'm spinning and scared shitless. Fuck, she's right. We've said all along that we'd just be friends with benefits, but somewhere along the way, maybe even before we started having sex, I think, it got more serious. I haven't been with anyone else since we started working on her house weeks ago, haven't even thought about it because Cassie was all I needed. I wake up looking forward to the day, telling myself each time that it's because I enjoy the project out at 614 Douglas. But that's a lie. I've been looking forward to the time spent working with Cassie. I've been looking forward to spending my time with her. Even the nights when I've gone over there exhausted, I feel good because I've been doing things for her.

What the fuck am I gonna do now? I don't want the whole relationship thing. I obviously suck at them, if history is a good example. I can't give my heart to someone again just to have it stomped on.

CHAPTER 24

CALEB

I've spent the last few days working like a madman, sunup to well past sundown. The only breaks I've taken have been to force myself to the gym for intense but abbreviated heavy workouts, throwing weights up and letting them slam to the ground in a misguided attempt to let off some steam. I'm trying to keep my mind busy, and it at least serves as a temporary distraction. I'm not sure what is going on in my head, and I'm not sure I'm ready to face it either, so I'm just gonna avoid that train wreck and work myself to death.

Cassie's called me twice this week, trying to get together, and I've told her that I needed to get some stuff done on her house because materials are being delivered and I have to be ready, plus, I have another job that needs some attention too. She offered to come help, but I was a bit of a shit and said I could do it faster alone. The obvious truth is that I just need some space because I'm freaking the fuck out. It makes me feel like a total asshole, not being honest that I need a moment to get my damn head right. I mean, I know her history. She's probably thinking I'm just like those assholes who ran out on her mom. I swear I'm not, but I just need to think!

So here I've been, working myself to the bone, not going home until ten or later every night. The results are clear, though. The house looks fantastic, if I do say so myself. The texture dried quickly in the summer heat, and while it set, I was able to do the floors. Cassie ordered a rich deep chocolate brown stain for the floors, which went on beautifully before I applied a sealing coat of poly.

I questioned her on her idea for wood floors in the bedrooms, but she said people would put down rugs by the beds for toasty morning toes. Those were her exact words, "toasty morning toes," and at the time, I laughed at her. But I miss her silly ways of saying things.

Fuck, man. Stop it . . . focus. That wasn't the deal, remember?

Today, I'm painting the upstairs bedrooms and super-vising the crew I hired to come fix the porch. While I probably could have done the job myself, it needs to meet codes for listing, and the amount of wood and the lengths involved were a lot for me to handle on my own. With the need to bed the posts in concrete foundations, it was easier to outsource the job, and it gets this project closer to the finish line. Besides, I know these guys and I know they will do the job right.

I work through the entire morning, and in mid-after-noon, I stop to eat lunch, double-checking my work as I inhale my third peanut butter and jelly sandwich. The dove grey color looks as great as Cassie predicted, giving a softness and warmth to the rooms the bare white didn't have. She teased me about the paint too, saying she was gonna go hit up John at Home Depot to see what he recommended because she was certain he'd have some interesting ideas in that orange apron of his.

Thankfully, though, in the end, she went to the specialty paint store I strongly recommended. But the tone is just right, and it compliments the entire motif of the house, lots of blacks and whites, with the grays acting less like depressing tones but more like light that'll catch the sun coming through the open windows to soften them. There are also enough little details that add to a general tone of calm cheer that the house looks like it'll have an aura of peaceful warmth and splendor, if the owners can furnish it right.

As I wander through the rooms, I hear a car door close out front and the porch crew guys talking to someone. Wondering who it might be, I head downstairs and to the front door, freezing when I see Cassie.

Shit. Just be cool. It's only Cassie. We're just friends.

Just a friend? A friend you've seen naked more times than I can count and know just how and where she likes to be touched. Face it, idiot. She's got what you need, and you say she's just a friend.

Cassie sees me through the open door and smiles, lifting her hand in a wave. Coming through the door, she ignores the work crew and beelines right to me. "Hey, Caleb. What's going on, stranger?"

She goes to hug me, but it's awkward when I don't hug her back, just giving her shoulder a little pat. She gives me an odd look and I try to explain. "Paint . . . not sure if it's all dry. I don't want to get you dirty."

Cassie steps back with a teasing smirk on her cute, bow-shaped lips, and I feel myself more torn than ever. "You sure didn't mind getting me dirty before."

She's joking around, trying to banter like before, but my heart's not in it right now. Instead, I shrug, trying to find something to say that doesn't make me look like an asshole or an idiot. Sadly, I fail miserably.

"Yeah, uh . . . good one." Gesturing to the back of the house, I ignore the questioning look from Cassie and start talking. "Come here and let me show you something. As you can see, I got the wood floors all stained and a coat of poly on them. They say you don't even need to wax them, so that'll be nice. Oh, and yesterday, I got the floor tiles done in the bathrooms. I've been painting this morning— the upstairs bedrooms—and by the end of today, I'll have the hall done too. Tomorrow, I'll either start the bathrooms or the kitchen, depending on the delivery today. Bathroom stuff is here, but the cabinet fixtures are set for this afternoon, and if I can get those in, I'd prefer to do that. So if they get here early enough, I'll focus on that." I'm rambling, talking about stuff she already knows. Hell, she sent me the delivery dates on the materials. After all, she put all the orders on Oliver's company credit card.

But I don't know what else to say. I just need to get us back to before somehow. I want to go back to where I can look at Cassie and just see my friend, the girl who sure is hot as fuck with a body that has pleased me like nobody else. But it's really her heart and smile that warm me, make me want to be her friend, and more . . . *wait, fuck*.

Cassie looks at me for a moment, finally speaking up. "Sounds good, I guess. Got everything you need? Need any help with paint? I'm pretty much a Picasso when it comes to painting, or we could split it up . . . you roll and I'll do the trim?"

Trim? When she says it, all I can think of is how it would feel to take her upstairs and check on *her* trim. My hands start shaking, and I shake my head quickly, hoping that I can get this over with before I make any more of an ass out of myself. "Nah, it's okay. I know you're busy. I've got it under control. That's what I get paid for, after all." I know I sound dismissive, and the air surrounding us feels uneasy, awkward with tension and I know it's my fault.

"Mmmhmm," Cassie says quietly before clearing her throat. "But this is my project."

I don't have a reply, the weight in the room dragging down, but after a moment, she shrugs. "Okay. Well, I'll get out of your way then."

She turns around and adjusts her bag strap on her shoulder, almost as if she's waiting for me to say something. At the bedroom door, she stops before walking out, pausing and looking back at me. Her voice sounds strained, and I can see her eyes glistening. I won't allow myself to say that they're tears. "Hey, Caleb? I want you to know that it's okay if you're swimming. I get it, but I still want to be friends."

Before I can reply, she walks out. I hear her holler goodbye to the porch guys, and as she pulls away, I can hear them trash-talking about how hot she is, and it pisses me off so badly that I want to go out on the porch and bust every single one of their disrespectful asses right in the mouth. But I don't have any right to be mad and I know it, so I turn my radio full-blast and take my frustration out on the bedroom walls, covering them with the ugliest fucking grey paint I've ever seen.

Metallica's Unforgiven serenades me as I wonder what the hell's wrong with me. Not that the paint has any answers.

CHAPTER 25

*F*uck. Fuck. Fuck. What happened? I thought everything was going pretty well. We were getting along and the sex was beyond amazing. Sure, we were getting a little closer than being just fuck buddies, but so what? It seemed to me that Caleb was cool with it and we were just adapting to a new situation. Apparently, everything *wasn't* cool, because Caleb is acting so distant, even not-so-subtly trying to get rid of me.

I don't know what I did. Last time we were together was awesome. He even slept over and didn't seem weird when he left that morning. I mean, it wasn't like I cleared out space in the medicine cabinet for him to leave a toothbrush or tell him that he could use one of my drawers to keep a spare pair of jeans and underpants. We just had sex, and it was late so he slept over. Yeah, things got a little emotional afterward, but it was still cool. At least, that's what I thought at the time, but then he pulled that ghost job on me for the rest of the week. What could've happened?

Damn it, I know better. I shouldn't be asking what happened. The better question is, *who* happened? He's met someone, and he doesn't know how to break the news to me. He knew inside as much as I did that we've crossed a line, even if we weren't sure what the hell to call ourselves anymore.

It's just what I've come to expect, I guess. Mama always told me to be careful, because even if what's at home is great, men will scout for the next one. Okay, so he's swimming away just like I assumed in the beginning. He's too good of a guy to keep up this casual sex thing. I knew that even before we started fucking around. He deserves more than a setup like that. I knew better than to get attached, but I fucking went and did it anyway. When did I fall for him?

I stop, looking at myself in the bathroom mirror, my toothbrush dropping to the countertop where it tumbles into the sink, unnoticed. Instead, I look at the haunted face of the woman staring back at me with puffy bags under her eyes, hollowed out cheeks from not eating enough the past few days, and . . . the realization hits me like a punch between the eyes.

Oh, shit. I *have* fallen for him. This is bad. I told myself since leaving home that I wasn't going to let this happen, that I was going to focus on my career. Now, without even realizing it, I let Caleb in and it hurts so much.

Why did it have to be Caleb, of all people? He's a man I

like, not just as a man, but as a person too. I don't have many friends. The list of people I really trust can be counted on one hand. And Caleb was like the thumb of that group, the one I could always count on to be strong and there for me. And I went and fucked it up.

I take a big breath. "All right, Cassie, get it together. You'll get through this," I tell my reflection. "Chin up to see the sun lighting the way, just like Mama always said. Appreciate the good and it'll get you through the bad," I add. "Maybe this is just a little phase. Once he's comfortable, everything will be back like it was before. We can laugh and talk and . . ."

Before the tears can start, I stop talking, trying to think of what I need. What I need is to get my mind off Caleb Strong. And right now, the only thing I can think of to do that is to work. Yes, that's it. I'll go to the office. I've got stuff to do and the distraction will do me good. I quickly get dressed, casual today since, quite frankly, I don't feel like putting on a skirt and Oli doesn't care how I dress unless I'm meeting clients. With barely a last glance in the mirror, I grab a granola bar and jump in my car.

Pulling into a space at Mindy's Place, I barely have to debate before I head inside. If I'm going to get through the day, I'm going to require mass quantities of caffeine and maybe the addition of a lot of forced humor. As I wait in line, I think about what I'm going to do to distract myself. I've just gotten to the idea of seeing if I can fit my entire ass on the copier before I order my drink and sit down at a vacant table in the corner, trying to hide. Both literally and figuratively.

It doesn't work, as I see Martha picking up her cup of coffee and mine to head my way. She looks like she's already had her high caffeine enema for the morning. She's smiling and looking like she's ready to take on the day. She's dressed up a bit, wearing a pantsuit that flatters her, honestly. It makes me feel even worse, looking down at my khakis and quickly pulled-on red blouse. Ugh.

"Hey, Cassie! I called from upstairs to order my cup of joe, but Mindy asked if I could bring yours on over. You mind?" she asks, gesturing to the empty chair in front of me. I'm used to her being nice, but there's something in her voice that makes me on edge, like she's sort of engineered this and is looking for a reason to talk.

"Of course not. Sit." What am I gonna do? Tell her no, go away, I want to be alone? Hello, Captain Obvious, I do that and she's for sure going to know something's wrong. Instead, I plaster a fake smile across my face. More than likely, she's going to give me a 'talk', and right now, the last thing I want is a talk.

"So what's going on with you, Martha? Find any good properties to consider lately?" I ask, desperate to keep the conversation off me and more on business. "I can do drive-by checks if you need some help." *I need something to keep me busy, dammit!*

Martha shakes her head, leaning back and crossing her legs primly before giving me a rueful smile. "No, dear. I'm afraid that Oli's got me looking at commercial properties for a client right now, not for his own investment. So I'm working directly with their management team to find the right place. Thanks for the offer though. I haven't seen much of you lately. How's your house project going?"

"Pretty well. The demo and reconstruction are done, including the electrical and plumbing. The new porch is in, and by now, the painting should all be done too. All that's left are the kitchen and two and a half baths, and then I'll stage it for sale. Comps are looking good and we're under budget just a little, so that helps with the tight profit margin."

Martha gives a little hum. "It does sound like you've got it well in hand, Cassie. Congrats on doing such a great job. I know Oliver had some worries about it, but it sounds like you'll do fine. How's it been with Caleb? Y'all are always a hoot to listen to when he comes in the office. Have you guys been able to keep it, well, professional and friendly when the time's right?"

I can tell she's fishing, trying to pump me for information, but I'm not ready to go there yet. Instead, I stir my coffee, letting it cool for a moment before I take a sip, letting the bitter drink wash down my throat and hit my stomach. It's good, and I remind myself that before I head upstairs, I should probably get an iced one. Martha clears her throat and raises an eyebrow, and I know I can't delay any longer, so instead, I deadpan, "We're doing fine. We've managed to wrangle our incessant need to bicker and have gotten stuff done. It's been . . . fine."

Martha gives a soft laugh. "Nice try, Cassie. Try again. In the fif—well, the more years than I'd like to admit being around, never have I known a woman to use the word *fine* to actually mean fine. Especially when it comes to men."

I give her a long look and finally just shrug. "I don't know what to say."

Martha sips at her coffee, the silence drawing out for a few minutes before she speaks again. "Cassie, you don't have to tell me anything you don't want to, but I'm always here to listen if you need someone. Don't let it shock you, but I have a little experience in matters of the heart and maybe even a bit of wisdom in this old body of mine if you ever want to pick my brain."

She sits silently, finishing her first coffee and ordering another as she waits. I fight an internal battle of whether to say anything. It's over, but it'd feel good to get it off my chest maybe? Finally, after Martha has her second coffee, I spit it out, and not quite like I intended. "I fell for him."

I expect condemnation, or perhaps sappy false pity. Instead, Martha sips her coffee before calmly commenting, "Well, normally, I'd say that's a good thing, but given the look on your face, perhaps not?"

"I don't know. I mean, you know how we were, and I know you sort of gave me a warning, but it's gotten . . . complicated," I reply tentatively, looking hopefully at Martha. Oh, God, I wish I had someone I could talk to about this, but Hannah's for sure asleep. It's like three in the morning her time or something. Mindy's cool, but she's also the boss's wife. And Emily, I still don't know very well. It's one thing to giddily chat with girlfriends about getting some, but quite another for them to listen to you whine when it blows up as it always does. I really do need to make some more friends instead of working all the time. So instead, I'm unloading myself on . . . well, my boss.

Martha sits back, sighing. "Complicated. So many things contained within a single word, and none of them easy to understand."

"You sound like you've had experience with it," I say, and Martha laughs darkly.

"Believe it or not, back in my wild days, we had sex too. Despite the shoulder pads and hairstyles. And I had my fair share of office romance back then, and some stories that I won't share since I still see some of those people around town. And it's still . . . complicated."

"Yeah, so that, and it was going well . . . but then he bolted. It's fine, that's what guys do. I'm cool with that. I understand that some men are the forever type and some aren't. But I guess I fell for him more than I meant to, and now . . . it just hurts because I don't want it to mess up our friendship. But don't worry, it'll be fine. *I'll* be fine." I force the corners of my mouth up to resemble a smile, but the look Martha gives me makes it feel even faker than it is.

"Cassie, I'm so sorry. But not all guys bolt. I'm not sure whatever gave you that idea. Maybe some do, but some stay forever. Maybe that's not Caleb for you, but it will be *someone* someday. So don't give up hope. And honestly, I'm not sure it's not Caleb. Maybe he's scared. I don't know the details, but that boy is a commitment phobe if ever I saw one. Actually, I know why, too."

"You do?" I ask, and Martha nods. "How?"

"Like you said, it's complicated. Town like this, word gets around. We might look like we're getting up in size, and I guess the university has something to do with it, but the long-timers, the folks who were born and raised around here or have lived here awhile, they still gossip. That, and Douglas Reinhart was the contractor who renovated my house. His workers did a lot of talking back around then. But they all said Caleb's a good man, and I've never seen anything to make me think otherwise. Give it time, honey."

With a pat on my hand, she gets up. "I'll be in the office all morning and on properties this afternoon. You call me if you need anything."

CHAPTER 26

CASSIE

*W*orried that Martha would mother me to death, I'm relieved when she let me be the whole day, and this morning was more of the same. Now it's lunch time, and my stomach growls for the new panini Mindy's chef made for today's special. I pick up my order, deciding to walk to the park to eat, and wave at Mindy as I step outside. As I do, I see Caleb at the corner of the building. I stop. He's looking so handsome. Today, he's in some camo pants and a black t-shirt, his scuffed work boots only adding to his gruff sexiness. He's smiling, and I take a step in his direction before I stop. He's talking to someone just out of my sight, and I duck back before he catches sight of me.

Maybe I'm just imagining things, but I swear his voice has that same sexy purring growl that sets my stomach on its head and my pussy on fire when he talks to me. But this time, he's not talking to *me*. "Yeah, that sounds good. I've got some work stuff today, but tomorrow night works."

Before I can even wonder who he's talking to or try to delude myself that what he's saying is totally innocent, I hear a woman reply. She's got a sultry voice, the kind that could melt butter from ten paces and is dripping with honey in the way that only a born Southern belle can do it. "Thanks so much, Caleb. It's been awhile since you've been by. It's really great to see you again."

Caleb sounds a little shy, but eager at the same time as he replies, "Yeah, I've been busy. A couple of projects have me working long hours. But tomorrow's good. I'll see you then."

I hear a smacking noise and feel my heart shatter into a million pieces as I realize they're kissing. That fucker, he couldn't have just told me that he'd met someone? I'm mad, I'm seeing red, and I'm jealous as fuck. Swimming away is one thing, but to just . . . oh, that son of a bitch, I'll have his balls hanging from my rearview mirror!

I peek out and see him close the door on a little red sports car and tap the roof of the car. As the car pulls away, I see a flash of blonde hair in the driver's seat. In an instant, I'm lost. I pop out of the little alcove I've been hiding in and stomp toward him. My pulse is pounding in my temples and my fists are bunched at my sides.

While I look like a sweet little girl and I've added quite a few layers of girliness on top of the tomboy I used to be, I can still get down and dirty when it's warranted. Caleb, of all people, should know that. And he goes and treats me like this? As I close the distance, I get a little louder than maybe I should be. "What the fuck, Caleb? You couldn't just tell me you'd met someone?"

Caleb turns, his eyes going wide as he's startled to see me and my anger at first. He stammers for a moment before he recovers, trying to put another one of those heart melting smiles on his face. "Cassie? What–what are you talking about?"

"Damn it, Caleb. I know we said casual, but I thought we were at least friends and you'd be nice about it when you started seeing someone. But you just dropped me like a piece of trash. I mean, ghosting me and acting all distant —that's fine, I guess—but why not just tell me you'd met someone? I guess it doesn't matter to you. You're just on to the next one. Does Sportscar Blondie know you're an asshole?"

"Sportscar Blondie?" Caleb says, trying to play like he's confused, like he doesn't know exactly who the hell I'm talking about. "Cassie—"

I'm not hearing it. I'm in full-on rage mode. "Don't give me your shit, Caleb. You've got her lipstick all over you. Before you try the confused act, maybe wipe the fucking proof off?"

He rubs at his face, trying to get the stain off but just smearing it more.

Not that Caleb cares. He's still trying to run his line. "Cassie, wait just a minute. You've got this all wrong. She's not—"

But my emotions are burning through me, and I'm yelling when I cut him off. "Just don't. I know better. I damn well *knew* better than to fall in love with you. Just—fuck It. Send me a fucking t-shirt."

I turn, bolting away toward my car. I'm already pulling out when he catches up to me. He grabs at my door, but I'm already in reverse and his hand does little more than squeal as his fingers try and get a grip. I hear him yell, "Cassie!" at me as I peel out of the lot and speed away.

"Doesn't matter," I whisper, choking on my own tears. I blink, desperate to get anywhere, my voice dropping to a harsh rasp. "The sun'll come out . . . tomorrow . . . bet your . . ."

CHAPTER 27

CALEB

I stare at the twin red lights of Cassie's brakes as she runs a stop sign, not caring in her haste to get away from me. Luckily for her, downtown traffic is light at this time of day, but it just leaves me more confused.

What the fuck just happened? Cassie was so pissed, and if anyone else had flipped their shit on me like that, I'd be running for the hills. But Cassie? God, she's beautiful when her eyes are flashing fire and her cheeks are all pink with anger.

The problem was, she caught me off-guard. I truly didn't know what she was talking about when she began screaming at me in the middle of the sidewalk. Even now, as the pieces start to come together, I'm still feeling stunned. Sportscar Blondie . . . oh, sweet hell. Never, in all my life, have I run into a situation like this. If I weren't in the middle of it, I'd swear it could never happen.

The door to Mindy's Place opens up, and Mindy peeks out the door, looking uncertain. "Uh, Caleb, everything all right out here?"

I turn and realize that everyone inside is staring at me. The advantage of having big glass windows—you get a front-row seat to any streetside action. At least Mindy looks concerned, not just drama-mongering. I'm half tempted to spread my arms and ask the people staring at me if they're not entertained. "No, I don't think so, but what the fuck do I know?"

Mindy, who's always been sort of a sister to me since I started working with Oliver, comes closer. "Wanna talk?"

"Nah, not right now," I reply, trying to save what little scrap of dignity I have left. I shake my head, "Listen, I just gotta take care of some work. Tell Oli I'll stop by later. I need to give him an update on the projects he's got me working on and turn in my expense statement."

I wave an apologetic goodbye and hop in my truck. I want with every fiber of my being to chase Cassie down and demand that she tell me what the fuck just happened, but I don't even know where she went. And I've got a busy day ahead of me. In addition to getting a delivery at my place for some supplies for Oliver's properties, I've got another job today, and then this afternoon, I have to get out to Douglas Street to check that the porch crew finished their work correctly.

I head to my house, calling Cassie multiple times, but it just goes to voicemail. I sit in the driveway at the house and text her as I wait for the delivery guy.

Call Me. Now.

When Cassie doesn't text me back by the time the delivery guy and I have finished loading his stuff into the back of my truck, I shake my head and head off to work. I get the first job, a simple gutter cleaning for a young mother, finished quickly, giving her toddler a half-hearted fist bump before she waves goodbye. Oliver's units are coming along well, and he's going to have no problems getting them rented out when the university students start coming back, and with the little improvements he's made, he's going to be able to get even more profit out of them.

After a quick lunch of grilled chicken breast salad, I head over to Douglas Street. As Cassie doesn't respond to me, I become a man on a mission, working harder and faster, my emotions giving me an endless amount of energy. I ignore my tired body and let all of my mounting frustration out in my work, and it feels like I'm a Marvel Hero or something. I become . . . Handy-Man.

I get all the cabinets installed, countertops and backsplash complete, and the appliances placed before I take a quick dinner break. If you can call it that—it's just a couple of meal replacement bars I barely even taste as I chew them mechanically in order to have the energy to keep working. Apparently, *confused and pissed* is a good work mode for me.

As I gnaw the last of my second bar, I check my phone again. Still no reply from Cassie. It's well after dark and I don't know what to do. She won't answer my calls, so I decide to drive by her house. Yeah, maybe it's a bit stalkery, but fuck, I need some answers. Grabbing my keys, I jump in my truck and head for her place, the radio off for once. I'm not in the mood for 'happy' music, and I don't have the time to change out my playlist. Instead, I focus on Cassie and the deep desire inside me to see her, to explain what happened, and to let her know the truth.

No dice. As I drive by her apartment, her car isn't there and my mind whirls. Is she trying to keep busy like me? Usually, Oliver doesn't keep Martha and Cassie this late, but then again, she might not be following normal protocol. I hope that's all it is because the thought of her talking to another man makes my blood boil. It seems I've become a little possessive over Cassie . . . just like she obviously has over me.

Fuck. I'm too riled up, and I used to know just the thing to calm me down. Once upon a time, I'd go grab a piece of ass for a quick pick-me-up, but the thought of that just turns my stomach. I haven't been with anybody but Cassie in ages. Hell, even when I've jacked off, it's been her in my mind every time.

There's really only one thing to do, so I go back to Douglas Street. At least working distracts my mind and tires me out, keeping me from driving all over town to hunt her down. When I get there, I take the time to load up a proper playlist for my mood, and as *Nine Inch Nails* and every other angry, confused piece of rock I can think of accompanies me, I spend all night—literally all night— working. I sand, I screw, I clean, and I varnish until it's all done. My body argues with me, complaining every step of the way, begging for some relaxation after working all day. I ignore its complaints, and by the time the sun rises, the last bit of work is done. The only thing left to do is the exterior paint, which I hired a crew to take care of, and they're coming in tomorrow . . . well, actually, today.

I do a last walk-through, checking the details of every bit of my work. Floors, walls, ceilings, kitchen, bathrooms . . . yes, both full bathrooms and the half last night, as my back and arms remind me. The gleaming chrome and steel fixtures are all watertight and won't crack this side of a meteor strike. I made sure of it.

I step outside, looking at the porch with its big support posts and painted deck. Once the exterior crew is done, it's going to be a whole new house, nearly perfect. It just needs a finishing touch, and I know just the thing.

"She was right," I say, my exhaustion not disappearing but at least feeling justified as I look at the house. All this place needs is a fresh start. She saw its potential long before anyone else did. She felt it in her heart, knew how beautiful it could be, filling in all its defects, fixing its cracks, and ending with something greater than the sum of its parts. I think somehow, she did the same to me without my even realizing it. While I've been busy completing jobs on a list, just a regular old Mr. Fix-It, not looking at the big picture, she saw me. My brokenness. And while it wasn't joint compound and a coat of paint, she fixed me. With her laughter, her joyful approach to life, her lightness . . . she fixed me. That thought settles into my bones, my heart, and I know it's true. She might not have meant to, and I certainly didn't mean to let her, but she's done what I thought no one would ever do. She's made me want to love again, to dream and to hope that there is someone for me, after all.

With a snap of my fingers, I know what I need to do now. I head through the house, determined to be at Home Depot as soon as they open, but before I can get to my truck, a familiar silver-gray Lexus pulls around and Oliver gets out, dressed for work. "Whoo, if I didn't see it with my own eyes, I wouldn't believe it," he says, checking out the house. "I have to ask, though—what the hell are you doing here so early?"

"Just wanted to get the insides finished up," I reply, coming over. I stop a few feet away, smirking tiredly. "I'd offer to shake your hand, but I don't think your expensive suit needs my funky ass anywhere near it."

Oliver chuckles, nodding in appreciation. "Okay. Well, can you show me the inside? I was hoping to get some photos up soon and get it listed. Didn't expect it'd be this fast though."

I nod, a sudden flash of inspiration going through my head. "Of course."

We go inside, and Oliver looks through room after room in wonder. "Remember when I said that if I didn't have my place I'd think of a place like this?" he says when we reach the master bedroom. "Check that. This place—I love it."

"It's a hell of a home," I agree.

He turns and gives me a curious look. "You gonna tell me

what's going on, or do I have to keep playing the coy guessing game?"

I wince, rubbing at the back of my neck. "Mindy told you, huh?"

"Well, Martha told me first," Oliver replies. "She was upstairs and heard Cassie through the window. She got to watch the worst of it. Apparently, there was quite the show."

"Very funny," I reply. I take a deep breath and tell Oliver the truth about what's been going on between me and Cassie. After I get to yesterday's incident, he whistles. "Yeah, so that's all it is, man. I just need to talk to her to clear things up. Have you seen her?"

"She'll be in the office later today," Oliver says. "Maybe you can talk to her when you come by to pick up your payment on the properties I've had you running around on?"

"Actually, I had another idea," I say, deciding to hell with it —I gotta jump in with both feet. "How would you like to save some money, get another property you can use for rent, and help me out?"

Oliver has a twinkle in his eye. Maybe he'll go for it. "I'm listening. What do you have in mind?"

CHAPTER 28

"**G**ood morning," I hear, rolling over on the big, fluffy sofa. I stayed at Mindy's house last night after being unable to even think of going back to work after seeing Caleb with Sportscar Blondie. Instead, I spent the day driving in circles, and I even took a walk through the park, which ended up making me ugly cry at the memories of my runs with Caleb through there. When a lady dug in her purse and offered me a crushed up tissue, I figured I'd had enough and tapped out. I sent Martha a quick text, telling her I was taking a personal day, and fled the park before I lost total control.

I was at least able to get control of myself in my car, taking deep breaths and listening to Roxy serenade me from my stereo. Thank God the girl sings more than love songs. When I was finally able to breathe without the intense need to hitch my breath and start sobbing again, I called Mindy from my car and asked if I could crash on their couch. She was totally cool about it, inviting me over to have dinner with the family.

Dinner was almost surreal, as everything just seemed immensely normal. They didn't say a word to me about Caleb. In fact, they didn't talk about work at all. I'm sure Mindy told him what happened in front of the coffee shop, but they gave me space. The conversation was about their kids, Emily's silly antics as she tried to take care of them, and their plans for their upcoming family vacation. It was wonderful to see, and I couldn't help but crack a little smile at how wonderful their lives seem.

Mindy left first thing in the morning, needing to get to the shop to open for the early morning coffee drinkers. Now I see Oliver adjusting his tie. "Hey," I mutter sleepily, getting up. "Sorry, I'll head for my place, get changed, and head to work."

"Chill out," Oliver says, giving me a smile. "You stay as long as you need, and I don't expect you in the office today. Martha and I can handle everything."

I lie back, smiling softly. "Mindy's lucky she's got you. And you're the best boss ever."

"I'll remember that when I don't give you a Christmas bonus or a raise next year," he joked before patting me on the shoulder. "Relax, hang out with Emily today, maybe binge-watch something on Netflix."

After Oli left, I tried to sleep a little more but just tossed and turned on the sofa. I thought I'd get up, but apparently, I dropped back off, because I open my eyes to see Emily sitting on the floor, reading something on a Kindle.

"Hey," I reply, stretching. "How long have you been here?"

Emily, who, as normal, is dressed in jeans and an anime t-shirt, chuckles. "About twenty minutes. Zach's sleeping still, while Leah is coloring and Trent's picking up his room."

I stretch again and sit up, ruffling my hair. "Good deal. So what's on your mind for today?"

"Just a normal day," Emily says. "I'll get Trent working on his pre-K stuff, and we'll probably play outside for a while, stuff like that. You sticking around?"

"I think I will," I reply. "You got coffee?"

"Pot's in the kitchen, Mindy's homebrew," Emily replied. "It'll be cold by now, but for getting your day going, it'll do the trick."

Emily's right, and a minute in the microwave doesn't hurt the flavor too much. She follows me in as I raid the fridge, finding some cheese and a box of Ritz in the cupboard. "Hey, mind if I ask?" she says as I cut the cheese.

"What's that?" I reply.

"I sort of saw what you were watching on Netflix," Emily said. "You're into reality shows?"

I grin. It's the last question I expected, but probably the one that I most need right now. "Yeah, one of my vices when I have the time. Don't tell me you hate them and only watch stuff like that." I nod toward her shirt, which has two fairies, three girls in ridiculous princess outfits, and a bunch of Japanese on it.

Emily checks out her shirt, laughing. "No, I just wear stuff like this because the kids like it. Actually, I'm kind of a reality TV nut. I always tell myself I'm going to stop, and a few hours later, I'm still watching. Everything from *The Bachelorette* to *American Ninja Warrior*. You know that one?"

"I know of it," I reply. "Haven't seen much, though."

Emily notices my reluctance and leans against the counter. "What's going on? I mean, I know you don't know me well. I'm not trying to pry or anything."

I sulk, going over it all in my head, trying figure out where I went wrong. Finally, I answer. "I guess you could say it's like reality TV. Like those ones where you know it *has* to be semi-scripted because of all the crazy shit everyone gets into?"

"I know exactly what you mean," Emily says, smirking.

"Imagine finding love in the most insane way possible. What would it be?"

Emily thinks, then chuckles. "Well, I could be in a life or death struggle and fall in love with the enemy."

I snicker, then sigh. "Kinda like that. It wasn't life or death, but it damn sure felt like it at the time. I met him on a beach that was straight out of a reality TV show. Then moving to town and being friends for nearly a year before something else happened."

"Caleb?" Emily asks, and I nod. "Last time I heard, you two were bumping uglies," Emily says, holding up her hands when I give her a surprised look. "Sorry, I try to watch it around the kids, ya know? You might have the prettiest downstairs in the world, for all I know."

I laugh but then sigh a moment later. "Okay, probably safer. But yeah. I mean, like I said before, it was supposed to just be a casual thing. Some fun, stress relief, and hanging out. It . . . well, I guess I changed. I started getting feelings and I didn't even realize it until it was too late."

"What happened?" Emily asks.

"It really doesn't matter much at this point," I say softly. "He moved on like we both knew would happen eventually. I'll be okay, but it feels like my heart is shattered. Not even broken, just dust."

Emily nods, letting me have a minute before replying. "If it helps, I kind of understand."

"Really?" I ask. "No bullsh—no bull?"

"Nope, no bull," Emily says. "Honestly, my entire life since puberty's been a story of looking for love in all the wrong places, or maybe the right places but always finding the wrong guy. I did the whole bad boy that I thought I could fix thing for a while and that *never* works, so I went the other direction. I somehow found the only church-going *male* librarian who was also the worst two-timing sleaze ball ever. He fooled me for way too long." I can't help it. I chuckle darkly. "Okay, I admit that's some bad luck there." "I just . . .I'd like a real guy. Someone sweet and nice, who treats me well," Emily says wistfully. "No more bad boys with six-packs." She says it with commitment but then smirks. "Although if my nice guy were built like Thor, I certainly wouldn't complain. That'd just be rude." "Thor?

213

Or Chris Hemsworth? 'Cause that I can get with," I say, smiling.

Right about then, Zach wakes up, and Emily goes back to take care of him. After she leaves, my black mood comes back, and I sigh, reminding myself *chin up*. I just have to get through today and not track down Caleb at Sportscar Blondie's house tonight. I don't want to make a fool out of myself. Again.

With a slight smile at the idea of being the jealous revenge chick on the news, I drain my coffee and curl back up on the couch. I don't get a chance to get into the TV, as the kids are out soon enough, and at Emily's suggestion, I start helping out. It's distracting and again pleasant and fun to play with them, especially the baby, who's just about the most adorable creature set on this green earth.

It's a couple of hours later, after lunch, when Oliver comes in with a smile. "How are you doing?"

I try not to hate him on sight, smiling happily, but I can't help but have it in for all penis-bearing members of the human race right now. So instead of replying, I growl slightly. Emily, who's reading with two of the kids, laughs.

"You're not gonna get much more right now," she says. "What brings you home early?"

"Well, I hate to be the bearer of bad news, but Caleb and I had a talk. He said he's been calling and texting you but you're not answering."

"I've just been trying to keep a civil head," I growl. "What's he want?"

Oliver's got a little smirk on his face, like he's got something going on. "He needs you to come by the house. It's done and you need to do a walk-through before I get it listed and release the last payment for his work."

"What? How could he be done?" I ask. I'd rather do anything right now. "I mean, can you do it for me? Please?"

He looks thoughtful for a moment, then shakes his head with finality. "Nope, this one's all yours. Start to finish, remember? You started it. Now go finish it."

Fire burns in the pit of my stomach, and I'm not sure if it's anger or fear, but I have no choice. With another growl, I climb off the couch, not even bothering to change out of my jeans or fix the half-tugged-out ponytail that I've been wearing since Leah decided playing tug-of-war with my hair is a 'game'.

Fuck Caleb. I'm not dressing up for his sorry ass. He sends Oliver to be a messenger to get me to the house. He wants to get paid . . . fine. I'll just go get this over with. My breath hitches, and I wipe away a stray tear. I'll be alone tonight and he'll be out on a date with another woman.

"Oh, Cassie?" Oliver says as I get to the front door.

"Yeah?" I say without turning around.

"Can you take this to him as well?" Oliver asks. I wipe my eyes again and turn, anger burning deep in my heart as I see Oliver, still with that same half-assed grin on his face, holding out an envelope.

I look at him for a moment, lost in anger. This is probably

215

Caleb's check for the work he's done. I know I'm wrong and the man deserves to be paid, but it just rubs me the wrong way.

"Do your job, Cassie," Oliver says, his voice becoming a little stern. "It's tough, but you can do it."

I take a deep breath and stare at him for a second. I want to tell him to take his envelope and shove it up his ass. I want to tell him that I quit, that this is the straw that breaks this particular camel's back. But I don't. Maybe there's a lesson in this, something Oliver's trying to teach me. Whatever it is, I can't see it right now, so it's better that I keep my mouth shut and leave. As the screen door slams, Emily calls out.

"Hey!" she calls. "Next time, let's watch *Dancing With The Stars* together!"

CHAPTER 29

CALEB

*M*y heart's pounding in my chest and my stomach clenches as I do everything I can to fight my nervousness, moving things a couple of inches just to move them back again. I'm hoping she'll come, but Oli wasn't sure if he could talk her into it. He promised not to give anything away. He said it was my right to tell Cassie on my own.

Listening to him this morning, I nearly threw up twice at how much I'd inadvertently hurt her. If I hadn't had an empty stomach, I probably would have. Apparently, she stayed on their couch last night. That fact, I'll admit, gave me so much relief Oli actually laughed out loud at the look on my face. He called it 'puppy dog eyes' and told me good luck. "Just remember," he told me as he got in his Lexus to drive to the office, "when she gets here, talk to her inside."

"Why?" I asked, making him laugh.

"So that when you grovel, you don't get a bunch of dirt all over yourself," Oli said, pulling away.

After showering and shaving, I wait with bated breath, hoping she'll show up. I'm sitting on the newly installed porch swing, pushing myself back and forth with one toe, when I see her car. One glance, and I know this is going to be even harder than I thought it would be.

Cassie pulls in the driveway, and I stand, frozen on the porch. When she steps out of the car, she doesn't even see me. I see her mouth fall open as she sees the tire swing I hung from the big tree out front, a big SUV tire that I suspended using nylon straps. It's not an old rope, but it'll last a lot longer, and I can see as she goes over and gives the tire a push that she's enraptured by it.

She looks a mess, a sloppy half-snarled ponytail sort of sticking somewhere out the back quarter of her head with tendrils escaping down her neck and bare face. Her jeans are a little big, barely holding onto her hips, and the faded tank top hugs her breasts. And she's never been more beautiful. No matter how angry she is, she's going to hear the truth. I have to get her to listen.

I approach slowly, scared that if I startle her, she'll run away. As I get close, I hear her whisper, "Perfect." Tears are running silently down her cheeks, and as I crunch over a dead leaf, she turns, her face still showing a hint of pain but her eyes glowing. "You—you did a good job."

I want to grab her in a hug, to tell her it's all a big mistake and to never let her go. I don't, though. I have to talk to her, heart to heart, first. "I wanted to make sure that this thing will be hanging up here for the next twenty years."

"So you overbuilt the shit out of it," Cassie says before giving me a weak, bitter laugh. "I wish I were this overbuilt."

"Cassie—" I say, but she interrupts me.

"Here," she says, reaching a hand into her purse and handing me an envelope. "Oliver said to give this to you."

I grin. I can't help it. *Oliver, you sneaky bastard.* "You sure? Open it."

"Come on, Caleb, stop fucking around!" Cassie cries. "I just want to get the walk-through done so Oli can list it! Take the envelope."

I take the envelope but keep my silence, trying to work past this bit of last-second fear. Finally, Cassie sighs and looks at the house. "I'll let him know it's done and that I gave you the check. The realtor comes by early next week to list it, so it'll be on the market soon."

I grin, feeling sheepish. "Yeah, um . . . I talked to Oliver about that. He canceled that appointment. The realtor isn't coming by."

Cassie looks shocked. "What? But he was just busting my chops half an hour ago telling me I had to see this all the way through."

I nod, reaching out to take her hand. "Cass, you said something when you were yelling at me the other day.

You surprised me and confused the fuck out of me. You said you fell for me."

"I did say that, but it was a mistake," Cassie says, trying to pull back, but I won't let her hand go.

"No, it wasn't. Because I love you too. Here." I hand her the envelope and then press the house keys into her hand, closing her fingers over it. She takes them with a confused look on her face, ping-ponging from the keys in her hand to my face.

"You love me? And . . . keys? What? And what's with the envelope?"

I feel light, as if a giant tie-down that's been wrapped around my chest were suddenly cut loose, and I take her hand again. "It's yours, Cassie. This house is yours—if you want it, that is. It's not a check in that envelope. It's the contract. It's the agreement I struck with Oliver. He and I worked it out this morning. He gets my house and your down payment, and the renovations I've done on his rental properties are free of charge for all the expenses he's incurred."

"But . . . but why?" Cassie asks. "Why did you do this?"

"Because someday, you're gonna be the one to give this house the family it always deserved, although I think you and your mama were family enough for it. And if you don't mind my being a bit presumptuous, I'd like to be the man to make that family with you."

Cassie's eyes are swimming with tears of shock, and her

voice is a choked whisper when she can finally reply. "But what about Sportscar Blondie?"

I step back, rubbing at my neck and laughing. That had been the hardest part to understand, once I really calmed down and set my mind to it. "Yeah, it took me a bit to figure out what the hell you were talking about. The blonde you saw in the car . . . did you see her before you went postal?"

Cassie shakes her head. "No, but I heard you and her, and you had her lipstick all over your cheek."

"Yeah, that's Mrs. Barnes," I reply, and Cassie blinks, realization starting to dawn on her once she hears the name. "I do work for her around her house sometimes. She's got a little crush on me and tried to give me a thank-you peck —that I dodged—and she caught my cheek. You probably know her. She's friends with Oliver's mom."

"Oli's mom?"

I nod, blushing a little "Yeah, a really sweet lady who's a bit lonely since her husband died and likes to flirt with me. She needs to have some work done at her place, and she makes the best lemonade and cookies I've ever had. I know you remember my telling you about that."

Cassie steps back, and for a long, drawn out moment, there's nothing but the trill of the cicadas until she leans back, laughing to the sky. It's pure, joyful laughter, and as she continues, I can't help but be drawn in by it until we're both leaning on the tire, our guts aching with rib-splitting bellows. Finally, when it hurts so much that even my stomach is cramping, Cassie gasps out, "Are you kidding me right now?"

I wipe at my eyes, shaking my head. "No lie. You wanna go with me tonight? I have to stop by there. It's a quick fix, just a leaky faucet. Maybe she'd knock it off a little bit if she met my girlfriend."

At the word *girlfriend*, Cassie stops, grinning. Coming around the tire, she leans in, running a nail across my chest as she peeks up at me. "Is that what I am? Your girlfriend?"

I nod, offering her my hand. "I love you, Cassie. Come on, let me show you the inside of your new house before we go see Mrs. Barnes."

She hesitates but takes my hand, pulling back slightly so that I look at her. "Caleb, I'm really sorry. I just . . . I was afraid. I thought you were like my mom's boyfriends, and I jumped to conclusions."

"You don't need to—" I start, but Cassie holds up a hand.

"You're nothing like them. I should've trusted you. You'd given me no reason not to, but it just felt so obvious at the time. I can blame my past, but the reality is that I blame myself. Really, I'm sorry."

I pull Cassie close, hugging her tightly. "I'm sorry too. Because I know what you mean. I was the one who was acting weirded out, and I'm sorry. But it's okay, and I love you."

"I–I love you too," Cassie says, trying on the words before smiling. "I like the sound of that."

"Me too," I say as I nod my head once at her, pulling her up the porch. She smiles at the porch swing, glancing back at the yard, and I know she's envisioning sitting here as her kids play on the tire. I hope that she's seeing the same thing I am, that I'm sitting there next to her and that it's our children out there.

We walk inside, and she freezes, her jaw dropping and her eyes lighting up. "Caleb, it's beautiful. It's everything I wanted it to be."

I nod, showing her the floors and the way the light through the windows makes the walls glow. I lead her into the kitchen, and she gasps, running her fingers over the butcher block island and turning the faucet on and off again. "I already called the water company. Everything's hooked up. You can start moving your stuff in tomorrow if you want."

"How'd you get it finished so quickly?" Cassie asks. I give a tilt of my head, and she follows me to the hall bathroom, our eyes meeting for a moment in the mirror.

"I realized I'd hurt you, and I'm not the sort of man who can use fancy words to say what's in my heart," I tell her softly. "So I poured it into this house, with my hands and my sweat. It's all here, my love in every board, every nail, every hour of work . . . for you. I love you, Cassie. I just don't know how to say it any better than that."

Cassie turns and puts her arms around my neck, drawing me in for a deep kiss. When we part, she's looking up into my eyes, smiling. "You said it perfectly."

We check out the bedrooms and the other bathroom,

finally heading back to the living room. "Caleb, it's amazing. Thank you. Truly. I hear you loud and clear in every detail. I'm surrounded by your love here. I want you to know I love you too. I didn't expect it, but I fell for you a long time ago. I started thinking of you, ways to get under your skin, maybe get under you, even. But it was more than that. I've loved you long before I even admitted it to myself. But . . . I love you."

Every time it rolls off her tongue, I feel my heart grow bigger, a knot that's been there for years undoing itself in my chest, and I hug her again, feeling her tiny body pressed against mine and the growing realization that I want to feel her in my arms forever. "I'm glad you like it. If there's anything you want changed or fixed, now's the time."

"No, it's even better than I hoped. But I do have a question for you."

"What's that?" I ask as Cassie gives me a knowing grin.

"You told me you sold your place to Oli. And you just gave me the keys to this place. So where are you planning on staying?"

Caught, I grin sheepishly and pull her close. "Well, I was kinda hoping—"

Cassie smacks me on the butt, growling lightly and grinning. "Oh, is that how you planned on it being? Well, tell you what. Let me think about it as we drive out to Mrs. Barnes's place. Maybe, just maybe, I might find an extra corner of a spare bedroom where I'll let you put a blanket."

"Is that how it's gonna be? But I love you!" I mock-protest, and Cassie laughs.

"You don't love me. You just love my doggy style. Now come on, before I'm too tempted by what I just said to let you get your work done."

I grin and check my watch. "Hmm."

"What?" Cassie asks, moaning when I reach out and grab her ponytail. "Your appointment . . .?"

"Gotta hurry or we'll be late, but when you make comments like that, you've gotta back them up."

Cassie gasps, reaching for the button on her jeans, grinning. "Yes, sir. So . . . are you carrying your protection?"

"I always have the right tools for the job."

CHAPTER 30

CASSIE

'm super-nervous as Caleb and I walk up to the front door of the small, neat house, but Caleb reaches out and takes my hand. "Hey."

"Yeah?" I ask, biting my lip. I took a few minutes to at least fix my hair, but I know I still look like a five-foot-one-inch pile of schlep, and I hate it. I'm here as Caleb's girl-friend. I'd rather be looking my best.

"You're beautiful," Caleb says, reading my mind. "Come on, let's just have fun."

Caleb rings the doorbell, and I have a quick half-second to tuck my shirt in before the door opens. I can tell Mrs. Barnes is surprised when she opens the door and sees me with Caleb, but she recovers quickly, going into hostess mode. "Caleb! I didn't know you were bringing a friend over too. I would've been more prepared."

Caleb gives me a little glance and a small smile as he

adjusts his tool bag that he's got in his other hand. I know what he's smiling about. Mrs. Barnes is rather dressed up for a widow who needs to have her sink looked at. In fact, she looks like she's about one set of five-inch heels from going out to a club to see if she can still work it low. "Sorry about that, Mrs. Barnes. I had plans with my girlfriend tonight and it's too hot to wait in the truck. I hope you don't mind."

Mrs. Barnes looks a little surprised when Caleb says 'girlfriend', and the word makes me feel like jumping up and down and screaming, *That's ME! That's ME!* "Caleb has just raved and raved about how you make the best lemonade and cookies he's ever had. Is it a secret recipe or would you be willing to share it?"

I have to give it to her. She recovers quickly, beaming at the compliment and ushering us into the kitchen. "Oh, no, I don't mind at all! I'm Sue Barnes, by the way."

"Cassie White," I reply, shaking hands with her. "I know this must come as a surprise."

"Only because I let myself be surprised," Mrs. Barnes says, chuckling sadly. "Come on, I've got that cookie recipe around here somewhere. Now, the key is, you have to use real peanut butter, not that junk they sell in the supermarkets."

As Caleb repairs the sink, just as quickly as he thought, I listen to Ms. Barnes discuss the pros and cons of different brands of peanut butter and even how to make my own to 'really get the best flavor'. I also get a quick little lesson on the best types of lemons, and how certain kinds are only available for a short season, and how to adjust based on the type of lemons you get. "But Mrs. Barnes, you say to drop the sugar?" I ask as I catch Caleb's eye, and behind her, he mouths *Thank you* to me.

"Oh, yes," she says, leaning in and dropping her voice. "Everyone thinks that you cover up the bad lemons with more sugar, but the thing is, you need to even highlight the lemons more then. So what I like to do is boil it."

"Boil it?" I ask, surprised.

"Boil, microwave, whatever you want," Mrs. Barnes says. "The lemons are usually too weak, you see. You have to bring the lemon flavor out, and the best way to do that is to steep the juices with the zest. Trust me, try it and you'll see."

"I don't doubt it," I tell her, liking her. She's a sweet lady, like Caleb said, and if she's into a little innocent flirting, so what? She even uses her home printer to make me a copy of both of her recipes, and I tuck them dutifully in my back pocket as Caleb cleans up. "Thank you."

"Hey, Cassie," Mrs. Barnes says as Caleb carries his tool bag out. "Take care of him, okay? He's a good man."

I nod, smiling. "You have no idea. Again, thank you."

After we say our goodbyes and Caleb tucks his check into his wallet, we go back to his truck, pulling onto the main street. "So . . . dinner? Feeling anything in particular?"

I lean back, rubbing my tummy and chuckling. "Caleb, I

ate like four cookies while Ms. Barnes talked about sugar brands. That woman had fully prepared for you. She had a whole plate and a half and two different types of lemonade. I can't eat another bite right now."

"Well, I'm starving," Caleb growls lightly, and the tone in the truck cab changes in an instant as I feel desire pulsing off him in waves. Who cares if we had a quickie right before coming over? We've held back for a few days, and we want each other *now*. I reach over, sliding my hand up his thigh to cup his hardening cock, and give him a cheeky look. If anyone ever asks me what love and true desire are, I can describe how Caleb is looking at me right now. I look like a half-kempt cocker spaniel and I can tell he wants to park the truck and make me scream his name. That's true desire.

"Well, maybe just a little more. But only if you can get us to my apartment fast enough." Caleb speeds up, virtually squealing into a parking spot at my apartment. He runs around to the passenger side as I climb out, turning to offer me his back.

"Hop on," he says, "or do you want me to carry you in my arms?"

I laugh and hop onto his back. "You can do that when you put a ring on it," I tease him, Caleb stopping for a half second in surprise before he grins and runs with me piggyback to my door, crouching down so I can feed the key into the lock.

Kicking the door closed with a foot, he sets me down. With a smirk, he growls, "Woman. Bed. Now."

I laugh, recalling how I teased him about being a caveman, but I run toward my bedroom, tugging at my shirt and getting it off before throwing it over my shoulder. I hear his muffled curse as it hits him in the face—he's so close on my heels—but when I turn around, he's not laughing. Instead, he's staring at me with a fire in his eyes that could melt steel, his chest heaving so hard that the thin cotton of his t-shirt can't hide the pounding of his heart, and his jeans certainly can't stop the bulging throb of his cock. "Fuck, Cassie. Strip for me, honey. I need to be inside you."

I feel his need and it's mirrored by my own, and I quickly start shucking clothes. In record time, I'm down to just my bra and panties. Baggy jeans have their advantages. "Like this?"

"It's a start," Caleb says as he turns around, going over to my drawers and opening my 'fun time drawer'. He reaches inside to grab a condom and looks back at me with an evil smirk. "Pick one. And tell me what you want."

"Ooh, the options, the ideas." With a smile of my own, I walk over next to him, letting my imagination run wild. I grab a few little things, setting them on the bed beside me before I turn and perch myself on the edge of the bed, my legs spread and my hands on the mattress behind me, showing off exactly what I know Caleb wants.

"Now, my stallion, take your clothes off for me." As Caleb reaches behind his neck to grab his shirt, I start to unbuckle his belt, teasing it out as he peels his t-shirt off until he growls, knowing I'm playing with him. He's so impatient he finishes it for me, shoving his pants and boxer briefs down as he pushes his boots and socks off. When he's naked before me, I take a moment to enjoy him, just letting my eyes run over every inch of him from top to bottom, then returning my attention to his cock, which stands hard and proud right in front of me. "Yep, you certainly like what you see."

"No, I love what I see," Caleb says softly, lifting my chin. "I love you."

"I love you too," I reply before reaching out and taking his warm, heavy cock in my hand and grinning. Caleb grins as I lean forward, giving the tip a little lick and looking up at him. "Do you trust me?"

Caleb raises an eyebrow, smirking. "It makes me a little nervous when you say it like that. But yeah."

"Good. I had a new . . . fantasy that I wanted to explore with you." I take the cock ring I got free with a purchased item on my last order, holding it up for him. His eyebrow goes up another notch, but he says nothing as I add a drop of lube, slipping it down over his cock, almost instantly seeing how much stiffer he's gotten with the slightly restricted blood flow. Caleb watches me with a glazed look in his eyes as I kiss and lick the tip of his cock, a slight moan coming from deep in his chest before I pull back, grinning. "Have you ever used one of these before?"

Caleb takes a deep, shuddering breath before he can answer. "No."

I give light little touches all along his shaft, and he shivers again. "It's to make you stay extra-hard for an extra-long time. You know why that's good?"

I let go of Caleb's cock to undo my bra, giving him a moment to recover as I free my breasts before pushing my panties down my hips. He smiles as I display myself for him, his cock now an almost cute shade of pink he's so hard. "Well, I can imagine the benefits."

I move to little lapping licks along his shaft, pausing periodically to talk dirty to him. He makes me want to be so naughty. "You said to tell you what I want. Well, what I want is to suck your cock, take you deep in my throat. But you're not gonna come that way, okay?"

Caleb puts his hand on my head, his fingers tightening in my hair. He's so on the edge, but he doesn't push, doesn't force me. He just lets me know that he could if he wanted. "Cass, I'm about to fucking come just from your talking to me like that."

I stop licking, letting his pulsing cock rest against my cheek as I look him in the eye. "I'm going to suck you, but you're not gonna come down my throat. When you get close, I'm gonna stop, and you're gonna work that dildo into my pussy or my ass—your choice. Your cock goes in the other, so . . . think you can handle that?"

I don't let him respond. From the look on his face, I can tell the answer. With a glint in my eye, I take his cock in deep in one fell swoop. He groans, reflexively grabbing my head with his hands and throwing his head back with a loud groan.

"How in the fuck did I get so damn lucky? Fuck, Cass." I continue to suck him, slurping and hollowing my cheeks to drive him wild. As I swirl my tongue across the tip, dipping into his tiny slit, he hisses. "Fuck, wait. Stop. I'm about to come."

"Well, we can't have that, can we? Not until you fill me up."

"Damn right," he growls, regaining his composure and his control. He pulls his hips back, and I can see the pulsing through his shaft. So close. Caleb half-squats, grabbing my hips before pulling. "Scoot to the edge." He pushes me back, bringing my ankles to his shoulders. I feel open, exposed, and totally turned on as he stares at my pussy, soaked and glistening with wetness. He dribbles a bit of lube on his fingers, rubbing my tight asshole with them, spreading the lube. "Now it wasn't one of your choices, but I need a fucking taste of you."

I grin, grabbing my ankles and spreading myself a little wider. I hadn't thought of it either, but now that he mentions it . . . "As you wish." With the moan of a famished man seeing his first meal in days, Caleb devours me, slipping his tongue in and out of my pussy before settling down to lick temptingly at my clit.

All the while, his finger slowly moves around, relaxing me and finally slipping inside to stretch me. I gasp. It's been a long time since I've had anything back there, and knowing that it's Caleb makes it all the sexier. "Cass . . . my turn. I'm gonna lick you until you're right on the edge. But don't you fucking come until you're full of cock. Got it?"

I writhe, incoherent, but something he hears in my

nonsense must sound like an agreement, because he smirks and dives back in. I'm crying out in pleasure, hands threaded through his hair as he licks every inch of me, even teasing my ass with both his fingers and tongue. I'm right about to fall off the edge when he stops. "Caleb!"

"No, no, no. Not yet," he teases as he brings his cock to tempt my tight hole, prepped and ready for him. I close my eyes, willing my body to relax, and he grunts, slipping the head in and pausing to let me adjust. It's overwhelming. I feel like I'm being torn open, he's so thick, but at the same time, I need him. I take deep breaths, letting it flow over me. The whole time, Caleb stays totally still, giving me the time I need to relax. After a moment, I need more and move myself along his shaft, letting him in deeper and deeper. I open my eyes, smiling at him, and reach down and take his hand. He groans as he sinks in deeper, filling my ass completely. he's huge, but it feels so good. "Cassie . . . damn, baby, you're so tight. Fuck, you feel so good."

He thrusts gently a few more times, making sure I'm comfortable, and then starts to plunge in with more power. My vision swims as I feel his hips start to smack against my ass. I'm losing it, and it's only when Caleb stops that I can even understand what he's saying, focusing on the naughty grin on his lips. "Hand me the dildo, Cass. I want to see you completely full. See if you can take it."

"That's my handyman, never leaving a job half done," I rasp as I hand over the dildo, not needing any lube since my pussy is dripping wet. Caleb pauses his thrusts into my ass, slowly sliding the dildo into my pussy to the hilt, and we just freeze, our eyes locking, and enjoy the moment. I've never felt this full, my body or my heart. He begins to drive into me again, sometimes at the same time with his cock and the dildo and sometimes alternating. Not knowing what to expect is driving me wild, and he works to keep me pinned to him.

"Fuck, I can't hold out much longer. I'm gonna fill your ass up. Is that okay?"

The idea of feeling his seed deep inside me is perfect, and the only thing that could make it better would be to feel him in my pussy. The little voice in my head, the part that whispers about my biological need, says to me that this man could breed me and I would love every second of it. "Fuck, yes. Do it, Caleb."

He nods, thrusting hard and fast into my overloaded body. I can feel him swell, and he grunts deeply. "Touch your clit for me. Come with me."

With barely a strum across my clit, I detonate, bucking and screaming. Barely a breath later, Caleb joins me, yelling out my name as I feel his heat filling my ass and it sets me off again. We writhe together as long as we can, finally stilling and breathing heavily. Caleb, his breath still gasping, pants. "Holy shit, woman. I think I saw a bright light."

I smile, giving a little laugh. "Me too. Got a question for you though."

Caleb slowly pulls out of me, chuckling. "What?"

"What are you gonna do to top this?" I ask teasingly as he heads to the bathroom. I hear him laugh, and he comes back a moment later with a warm wet towel, helping me clean up. "What? I'm a very demanding girlfriend."

"I'll think of something," Caleb teases. "I'm going to be all you ever need."

CHAPTER 31

CALEB

After a shower, we collapsed into bed, crashing in post-orgasmic bliss. Her bed is perfect too, and I already know that when we move things into the house, this is the bed I want in the master bedroom. My bed literally feels like sleeping on rocks compared to this. Or maybe it's just that Cassie is right next to me, and it feels perfect.

I woke up once in the middle of the night to find her sprawled across me, head on my chest, leg thrown over one of mine and a hand fisted in my chest hair. She was pulling, obviously caught in some sort of dream as she growled in her sleep, and I wondered if she was kicking ass or taking names. Thankfully, brushing her hair off her forehead relieved her enough that she let go and I could fall back asleep, pulling her close to me.

The sun is barely rising now. I stir, stretching out and just looking at Cassie in the soft morning light. She's angelic, and I realize that somehow, in a way that I'm still not too damn sure I understand, I've found the perfect woman for me.

I kiss her lightly on the temple and ease out of bed, heading for Cassie's kitchen. In the cupboard, I find the first thing I need, and after raiding the fridge, I find the rest. Smiling, I get to work, not even worrying about putting on any clothes until I hear a warm chuckle behind me.

"You do that, you're going to end up with hot bacon grease on your dick."

I glance over my shoulder, seeing Cassie leaning against the doorjamb, looking like the world's cutest sleepover attendant in a football jersey—Gavin Adams, of course—and nothing else. It falls below her hips, and I wonder if she's got any panties on underneath that nylon. "Damn, I wanted to surprise you. Did I wake you up?"

"Well, I had this big warm teddy bear in bed with me, and when I rolled over, it was gone. But I could get used to this sight."

I laugh, smiling so hard it damn near cracks my face. "Go chill out or snooze for at least another thirty minutes. I barely have the waffle batter done."

"You're making me waffles?" Cassie asks, impressed. "I didn't even know I had a waffle iron."

"You didn't. Okay, off to bed again, wench!" I cry, brandishing my spatula.

Cassie looks down to between my legs, licking her lips. "As long as you don't burn my dessert," she says, turning around and giving me a peek at her ass that proves she's not wearing anything under that football jersey.

I take my time, making sure everything is perfect on the plate before setting it on the towel-covered cookie sheet. Cassie sadly lacks any sort of TV tray. I carry it into the bedroom, where Cassie is leaning back against the pillow-covered headboard, the jersey pushed up dangerously high.

"Damn, woman, you're gonna make me balance this tray with three body parts if you sit around like that."

"Like what? This old thing?" and with a pouty lip, she slowly swirls the hem up higher and higher on her legs, just teasing me with a hint of her sweet bare pussy.

I groan, getting closer to the bed. "My lady." I offer the makeshift tray.

"Breakfast in bed?" Cassie squeals, clapping her hands. "I thought you were going to call me out to the living room."

"Well, special occasions call for special efforts," I reply, carefully setting the tray on her lap. "Now, gimme a minute to go get my food and we can dig in."

Breakfast is delicious, waffles drowned in butter and maple syrup, nearly half a slab of bacon each, and instead of coffee, I made chocolate milk. "Well, not what I expected," Cassie says as she sets her glass down, smacking her lips, "but I have to say, it goes well with it."

"I got the idea when I came in early to Mindy's Place the night after that bad storm last year. Front window was busted out so she closed the place, and she was experimenting," I reply. "Cookies n' cream frappe, which was great when they reopened. I helped with cleanup and the window, and Mindy gave me one with a bacon and egg sandwich, since she had to use the bacon before it went over. Best damn breakfast I'd had in a year."

"I'll have to thank her then," Cassie says, sighing happily. "So you say a special occasion, huh?"

"Well, saying I love you, our being an official couple, all that . . . yeah, waffles and chocolate milk."

We finish up our breakfast, and when I come back from dropping the dishes into the sink, Cassie's looking shy, like doubts might be starting to creep into her mind. Wanting to make her smile, I jump on the bed, pinning her and tickling her. She screeches and starts flailing crazily, and it's game on, tickle fight. We toss and turn, discovering each other's spots and laughing loudly.

Unfortunately, I should know Cassie better. She hates to lose and never fights fair. When I find that the backs of her knees are ticklish, she shoves her ass in my face while at the same time grabbing my cock, distracting me long enough for her to bury her lips on my belly button and blow a huge belly fart that leaves me gasping for breath. Finally, I cry out. "Truce, truce!"

Cassie stops. I've got her foot while she's got her other foot in my armpit, and I see her big true smile that fills my heart. "You called for it first, so the winner, AND STILL champion, Cassie 'Snow' WHIIIIIIITE!" She makes an echo sound like a distant crowd cheering, and I let it go on for a moment before making a honking sound like a horn interrupting. "What?"

"By the agreed-upon rules of the Marquis of Ticklesbury, when one party calls for a truce and it is accepted, only for the other party to renege on that truce, that party is henceforth disqualified. So, in fact, your true champion is Caleb 'Crusher' Strong!"

I give her a little jostle and she lightly slaps at my chest, and with a big sigh, we snuggle. Cassie nestles against my chest, sighing happily. "I'm gonna call for my rematch someday though. The Tickle Belt is defended under the twenty-four/seven rule, you know."

"I know," I joke, kissing the top of her head. "I'm looking forward to it."

"So, uh . . . now what? I'm your girlfriend for now, but what about—" Cassie asks, her worries only momentarily sidetracked by our tickle fight. I interrupt her before she can finish with a big kiss that shuts her up like a switch has been thrown.

"Cassie, you're my everything for as long as you want to be. Remember, I didn't run on you."

"What about that time I came by the house and you were acting all weird on me?"

I shrug. "Okay, point taken. But Cassie, I was trying to figure out what was happening. I mean, it wasn't long before that when we both said this was just a fuck buddy arrangement, and I realized the night I stayed here the last time that I was falling for you, and it scared the shit out of me, especially when I thought it was only on my side."

Cassie sighs. "This is all sorts of fucked up, you know that?"

I nod and turn to look her in the eyes. "Look, we've both got some issues, but I'm willing to trust that you won't stomp my heart if you're willing to trust that I'm not swimming away at the first available opportunity. I love you, Cass."

"I love you too," she says as she stretches up to meet my lips in a soft kiss, pulling back after a moment. "Deal. No swimming, no stomping," she says, pointing first at me, then at herself. "Now that's settled, what about the house?" Cassie asks. "I mean, you said you gave your house to Oliver as part of the payment for 614 Douglas."

"What about it?" I ask. "Cassie, I gave you the keys. It's yours. Sure, there's a part of me that's hoping that I can just move my stuff in with you. If not, I'll pay rent to Oli on my house until I can find another place. My address isn't important. You are. I don't mean to jump ahead of things, but I've been thinking long-term with us. Who knows? One day, maybe have a family and a dog. The whole fantasy . . . if that's what you want. It's what I've always wanted."

Cassie doesn't say anything for a moment, and I start feeling nervous until she gives me a smirk, biting her lip. "So, what are you doing tomorrow?"

I give her a look, my heart hammering in my chest. What I said, everything I did—there was always the chance to back out. Now there isn't, and Wendy Reinhardt's ghost tugs at me for a half second before I shove it away. This is Cassie, and I love her with all my heart. There's no reason to hold back. "Uh, tomorrow? Nothing, I guess. Why?"

"Well you said one day. How about we start tomorrow? We can move our things in and it'll be our house. Our home. I want that fantasy too, house, family, dog, all of it. With you."

"I think I can add it to my to-do list. Sounds like a plan. Gotta put my truck to work somehow." Instead of tickles, I attack her with kisses. She screams all the same, but this time, she's fighting to get closer to me.

EPILOGUE

CASSIE

*I*t's been six months to the day since we moved into *our* house. It still gives me chills to think of it that way. *Our* house. The house we tore apart, rebuilt, and created together. Somewhere in there, as we fixed the house, we fixed each other.

Sure, we've both had times when our issues have given us challenges. He understood, though, and in a move that might have taken a few extra hours and quite a few people by surprise, Caleb took me on a few visits to Ms. Steele's friends who wanted to fix him up with their daughters. We even developed an 'assistant costume' for me, a sports bra, a low-cut tank top, and coveralls that showed off all of my curves for any who didn't get the message by my merely showing up on their doorstep.

Actually, it led to one of our funniest incidents when the daughter, rather than getting the message that Caleb was unavailable, decided to hit on *me*. We both had a laugh after that, along with a night filled with passionate love-making where we got to use some of my toy collection in ways that we hadn't tried before. Exhausting, but fun, and I'm glad we skipped our Sunday run *that* morning.

Today, we're celebrating our half-anniversary the same way we do every night, swinging in the porch swing as the sun sets. It'll be too cold to keep it up soon, but for now, we just wrap up in a blanket in each other's arms and then head inside to warm up when it gets to be too cold. Caleb's taken care of it, of course, and we've got enough logs split and stacked to keep the brand new woodburning stove in the living room going every night we want.

Getting out of my car, I hurry toward the house, Caleb already waiting for me on the porch, blanket at the ready and a cup of cocoa waiting for me. I give him a quick kiss and run inside, changing hurriedly so I don't miss it. Dashing back out, he holds the blanket open for me, and I snuggle in next to his body, enjoying the heat he gives off as I try to warm up. As we sit, me curled up with my legs beside me and his arm wrapped around my shoulders so that I can rest my head on his chest to hear his heartbeat, he uses one toe to swing us slowly as the sun drops just below the horizon. Once the sun's disappeared and the sky is a single blaze of gold and red, he finally speaks. "So how was your day?" he asks.

"Good," I reply, nestling against him. "We got your old house rented out, by the way. A pair of students from the university. Oh, and that reminds me. He had a question for me today. What would you say about you and me partnering together on another renovation? I had my eye on a tri-plex."

Caleb raises an eyebrow. "Going into business for yourself?"

"No, I'll be partnering with Oli. You know I don't have the money to do it all myself. Yet."

"Well, that sounds good. But I had another idea," Caleb says. I smile and look up at him. He's holding up a ring, and my mouth drops open as I pop up onto my knees. "Really? Caleb? Oh, my God . . . yes!"

Caleb laughs, pushing my scrabbling hands away. "Cass, I haven't asked you anything yet. You mind if I do that bit traditionally?"

I try to calm down, really I do, but I'm buzzing with electricity inside as he takes my hand. Shrugging off the blanket, he gets off the porch swing and gets down on a knee. He clears his throat, and when he speaks, his voice is quavery, loaded with emotion and thick with feeling. "Cass, I love you so much. I didn't think I would ever take a chance on love again, but with you, I don't have a choice. I love you so much that I have to be with you. Cass, will you be my forever fuck buddy?"

The tears that have been pouring from my eyes stop in an instant and I push on his chest a little bit. "Hey, you'd better get serious before I take my biggest dildo to your ass!"

Caleb laughs, and even I have to crack a smile. Face it, that's just us. We're not going to have a typical marriage because we sure as hell haven't had a typical relationship. "Just kidding. Cass, will you do me the honor of marrying me? Will you be my wife and raise a family in this house with me?"

He slides the ring onto my finger, and I climb out of the swing, nodding happily. Jumping into his arms, I yell, "Now that's more like it! Yes, Caleb. Yes!"

He swings me around in his arms, twirling on the porch for a moment before setting me down and looking in my eyes.

"So . . ." he says, giving me a little smile. "What now?"

"Hmm . . . well, I can think of one thing," I tease, wrapping my arms around him. "I want to make love with my fiancé."

Caleb picks me up, this time cradling me in his arms and heading for the door. "You said when I put a ring on it, I'd get to do this," he says, and I'm touched that he remembered my little throwaway joke.

My heart swells as Caleb carries me through our front door and up the stairs, his strong arms not faltering as he lays me down on our bed. Stepping back, he gives me space to take off my clothes as he strips as well, standing at the side of the bed. His body is glorious. 'Domestic' life certainly hasn't dulled the sharp definition of his muscles one little bit, but it's the fire in his eyes that capture me as he looks me over.

Caleb swallows and grins. "I'm looking at my future, and it's the most beautiful thing I could have ever imagined."

I'm dumbstruck as Caleb climbs into bed next to me, his hand resting on my arm. Slowly, his fingers trace up and down my skin as we look into each other's eyes. I reach out, exploring the feeling of his skin, tracing the new tattoo he got last month, a rose wrapped around interlocked Cs along his left ribs. "You never told me why you put it here."

"My modeling career, of course," Caleb jokes, his hand traveling down to start stroking my breast in feather-light strokes. My nipple grows hard and pebbly, and he hums softly. "Actually, it's because when we snuggle, that's where you press against me. So even when you're not by my side . . . you're by my side."

I lean forward and kiss him softly, our lips and tongues caressing and melting against each other until my heart is racing and I feel something pressing against my thigh. Reaching down, I find Caleb's almost fully hard cock and grasp it, smiling against his lips. "I'm that good a kisser, huh?"

He grins at me and kisses down my neck, sucking and licking until he reaches my right nipple. I groan as he takes it into his mouth, sucking and licking until it's so intense I'm seeing stars. His hands stroke my back all the way from my shoulders to my ass, adding to the pleasure and making my pussy ache, wanting him inside me. Rolling him over, I straddle his waist, my pussy rubbing over the hard muscles of his stomach as Caleb's mouth feasts on my nipples. "God, I wish I were taller."

Caleb chuckles, knowing what I'm talking about. He's so tall, there's no way I can have both of my breasts sucked

251

LAUREN LANDISH

on and be filled with his cock. He pulls back, kissing up to my lips. "Cassie, you're perfect just as you are. I get to take my time pleasuring you from head to toe for the rest of our lives."

I look into his eyes, stroking his face as I rub myself back and forth over his skin, my clit electrified by the stroke of his hair over the sensitive bud. Caleb strokes back, kissing my lips and taking my breath away as I roll my hips faster and faster, my wetness smearing all over his skin and adding to the slippery sticky wonderfulness of it all. "Caleb . . . oh, God, baby."

"Any time you want, my love," he whispers, reaching down and squeezing my ass. I groan, squirming in delight as I feel him dip lower, his finger teasing my asshole until I relax and he slips inside me. I gasp, kissing him hard as Caleb slides his finger in and out of my ass while I grind my clit against him, fire building inside me until I have to push back, rolling off him.

"No . . . no, not this time," I gasp, immediately missing the feeling of his finger probing my ass. "Babe, this time, I want to come together."

Caleb nods, then smiles. "How do you want it?"

I get up on the edge of the bed, bending over and grabbing the blanket and grinning.

Caleb climbs behind me, running an appreciative hand along my spine before reaching up and grabbing my ponytail, tugging gently as I feel his cock slide between my pussy lips, not entering me yet but coating himself. I moan. I love feeling his strength and when he takes control because of how tender he is as he does it. "We get to do this forever," Caleb rumbles as he strokes his cock between my lips again and again. "I love you."

"I love you," I whisper. Caleb adjusts his hips just a little, and this time, his cock slides into me. I'm so wet that there's no tightness, just the amazing feeling of being filled by the man I love and the extra electric knowledge that there's nothing separating us. I look up at my hands, where my engagement ring twinkles in the light from the bedside lamp as Caleb starts stroking in and out of me. Each thrust of his cock is thrilling as he takes his time, bringing me to the edge time and time again before pausing, his cock throbbing inside me but not pushing us over into climax.

My body's shaking, the diamond on my ring twinkling as I flex and squeeze my hands, trying to hold on for what feels like the hundredth time Caleb's paused, grinding deep inside me while I back away from the edge. But I love it, the diamond hypnotizing me while I push back, squeezing Caleb and gasping. I feel his thumb rub over my ass, and I relax, knowing that whatever's going to happen, it's going to be the last climb.

"Fuu . . ." I groan as Caleb slips his thumb inside me as he pulls his cock back, pausing before stroking deep into me again. There's more power, less restraint this time, and I look over my shoulder, seeing the passion in his eyes. I'm enraptured as Caleb's hips slap into my ass, my body overwhelmed by the sensations as I give myself totally to Caleb and he gives himself totally to me. My pussy and ass squeeze around him, and Caleb shivers, smiling through the sweat glistening on his face and chest. We're both soaked, and he looks like something otherworldly as he speeds up, his balls slapping against my clit with every pounding stroke. I'm washed away on the wave of sensations flooding my body, and I bury my face in the blanket, closing my eyes. I can't take any more, except that it's Caleb, and I love him and—

My orgasm explodes through me, white-hot and lightning fast, seizing me in its powerful grip and not letting go. My heart, my lungs, everything stops as I'm rocked by the intensity, stars exploding behind my closed eyelids. I feel an instant of fear that I can't survive it, it's too powerful, I'm going to die . . . and then my ears catch the dim sound of Caleb's powerful roar as he comes too. The heat, glorious and completing, fills my body, and I realize that he's truly filling me, his seed granting me life again. My body shakes. I'm pushed even higher, but I feel totally safe and secure as Caleb's body collapses against mine.

He presses me into the bed, lying on top of me and letting his cock stay inside me as we relax, the sweat cooling on my hyper-sensitive skin as the cool evening breeze trickles in from the open window. Caleb wraps his arms around me and rolls us so that my nipples are teased by the breeze, and I shiver at the sensation. "My God."

"You are amazing," he murmurs, kissing my neck. "My love, my Cassie."

We lie there, our bodies still joined, and I smile, stroking my fingers over his forearm. "I love you too." I feel a twitch between my legs. It seems Caleb's recovered, and I laugh. "So, all I gotta say is I love you and—"

Caleb's cock twitches again, making us both laugh. "Guess so."

"Well, then," I tease, pulling my legs up and giving him better access while we lie on our sides, "I love you, I love you, I love you."

THE SPRING WEATHER IS JUST PERFECT AS WE GATHER IN THE backyard at Oli's place. While we wanted to originally have our wedding in the backyard at 614 Douglas, the winter rains showed us that unless we wanted my wedding reception to turn into a Slip 'n' Slide, it was probably better to do it somewhere else. After rejecting a humorous suggestion from Mindy that we have the reception at her place, or better yet, the Grand Waterways hotel, Oliver came to the rescue and opened up his house.

"Tell me that they've got a good DJ!" Ivy Jo, Mindy's grandma and unofficial comedienne for the whole event, says as she comes out of the house. "If I have to put up with one more bad karaoke from Jake, I'ma take my cane and shove it—"

"Grandma!" Mindy says, clapping hands over her son's ears. "Young minds repeat everything, remember?"

"Still . . . well, at least that damn yap bag isn't here. How'd I get so lucky?"

"I invited you because you were already going to be in town to see your great grandbabies and you're a sweet lady who makes me laugh," I tell her, coming out of the bedroom I've used to change into my reception dress. "What do you think?"

"I think you look lovely," Ivy Jo says seriously after another warning glare from her granddaughter. "But you won't stop all of my fun, Mindy. You know that right? I don't get out much these days, so I'm going to make the best of it."

"Don't worry, Ivy Jo," I reassure her. "Have all the fun you want."

I leave them behind, heading out into the living room where I see Emily, already changed and looking different than I've ever seen her before. Gone are the comfortable jeans and anime t-shirts, and instead, I see a beautiful young woman whom I've come to call my friend over the past few months as we've grown closer. It drives Caleb nuts, but it's fun to have someone I can watch all of my reality shows with.

"Hey," she says, smiling shyly. "You looked stunning in your wedding dress. Too bad you changed."

"I didn't want to get grass stains on it when I fall on my ass," I claim, laughing softly. "It's already been shrink-wrapped and environmentally sealed for when I have a daughter who needs it for her marriage."

Emily chuckles wistfully. "Yeah, well, it'd be nice to have that option." Emily, whose dating life has been even more of a bad luck story than anything I could have imagined, wraps her arms around her stomach and sighs, looking out at the backyard. "Sorry, don't mean to rain on your day."

I give her a side hug, smiling. "No rain at all. I'm glad you're here and not having to babysit all the kids."

"Sorta helps that Oliver's got a huge playset for the kids and Gavin loves playing with them too. Who knew a former pro football player would be such a great stay-at-home dad?"

The reception starts, and I'm surprised again as, instead of a suit like he promised, Caleb comes out of the house in a tank top undershirt, his tool belt, and his body glistening with sweat. "Oh, my, what's this?" Martha, who's my maid of honor and who gave me away at the wedding, says. "Caleb, I thought you were going to take the day off!"

"Decided to do a little more work," Caleb says, and the music starts up. I can't help but laugh as Caleb's followed out of the house by the rest of the men in our "extended" family—Tony, Oli, Jake, and Gavin—who are all dressed as construction workers-slash-strippers. Martha herds me and my friends into the front five chairs as the boys give us all a lap dance to *Work From Home*, culminating in Caleb's grinding on my lap to the point I'm tempted to cut the reception short and get right to the after party. He leans down, growling in my ear, "Apparently, this is some sort of tradition, according to Oliver. I can't break tradition, now can I?" And I bite my lip as I run my hands up the outside of his jean-clad thighs to his hips, mindful of the audience surrounding us.

Roxy, on the other hand, laughs and smacks Jake hard on his ass. "Work, work, work, work!" she howls, giggling. "I'm glad that I'm the dancer in our marriage!"

Caleb and the boys change into more normal reception clothes with scary speed, and I'm soon enjoying cake and toasts along with everyone. When Hannah gets up, my throat tightens.

"When I first met Cassie, the first thought I had was . . . how do I arrange to get my desk moved to the other side of the floor?" she says, making us all laugh. "Talk about a girl who would never, ever shut up!

"At first, I had reservations. Then, as we struggled together in the sands of Hawaii, I learned about a woman who is a fighter, a loyal companion, a woman with a heart bigger than her body and a spirit bigger than anyone I've ever known."

I'm barely holding back the tears when Hannah chuckles. "Then there was the night that I came back and there was this strange buzzing sound from her side of the room."

"Hey!" I call out, making everyone laugh. "You promised!"

"It was her alarm clock," Hannah finishes, making me blush furiously. "But that buzzing woke me up, too. Cassie stood by me when I risked it all for what was right, and I've spent every day since my marriage hoping that she'd find someone who loved her as much as I do. Thankfully, there was Caleb, who drove her just as nuts as she drove him . . . that probably should have been my first clue that these two were going to end up together someday."

"Or that they'd kill each other," Tony quips, and Hannah laughs.

"He's right. I'm glad they found happiness instead. So, to

Cassie and Caleb, may you find happiness in each other's arms, laughter in every day, and have lots of babies to snuggle. I know you've already found love."

The touching toast brings me to happy tears, and as the reception continues on to dancing, I feel swept away as Caleb and I dance together, the DJ playing Bon Jovi's *Bed of Roses*. I can't help it. I look up at my husband and chuckle. "Couldn't pass up the eighties rock, huh?"

"He recorded this in ninety-two," Caleb counters, smirking. "Don't worry, after this, I told the DJ nothing from before two thousand unless it's a ladies' choice."

"Good. Thank you, by the way."

"For what?" Caleb asks as we turn and move on the flagstones that make up the patio we're using as a dancefloor.

"For fixing me. For renovating my heart."

Caleb pulls me closer, smiling. "Time for renovations is over. I was thinking we could talk construction from now on. Our family needs an addition."

"I agree. Good thing I've already been working on that," I tell him, grinning lightly. "I was going to surprise you tomorrow with it, but you're going to be losing your home office, buddy. It's going to be the baby's room."

Caleb pulls me closer, and I can feel the wetness of his tears hitting my forehead. I hug him tighter, knowing that this leak doesn't need fixing.

Have you read all the current books in this series?

Irresistible Bachelor Series (Interconnecting standalones):
Anaconda || Mr. Fiance || Heartstopper
Stud Muffin || Mr. Fixit || Matchmaker
Motorhead || Baby Daddy

ABOUT THE AUTHOR

Join my mailing list and receive 2 FREE ebooks! You'll also be the first to know of new releases, sales, and giveaways.

Connect with Lauren Landish
www.LaurenLandish.com
admin@laurenlandish.com

Irresistible Bachelor **Series (Interconnecting standalones):**
Anaconda || Mr. Fiance || Heartstopper
Stud Muffin || Mr. Fixit || Matchmaker
Motorhead || Baby Daddy

Made in the USA
Middletown, DE
22 February 2023

25360351R00148